THE
BLACK
PEACOCK

A NOVEL BY

RACHEL
MANLEY

Cormorant Books

The publisher gratefully acknowledges the support of the Canada Council for the Arts
and the Ontario Arts Council for its publishing program. We acknowledge the financial
support of the Government of Canada through the Canada Book Fund (CBF)
for our publishing activities, and the Government of Ontario through the
Ontario Media Development Corporation, an agency of the Ontario Ministry
of Culture, and the Ontario Book Publishing Tax Credit Program.

LIBRARY AND ARCHIVES CANADA CATALOGUING IN PUBLICATION

Manley, Rachel, author
The black peacock / Rachel Manley.

Issued in print and electronic formats.
ISBN 978-1-77086-508-2 (softcover). — ISBN 978-1-77086-509-9 (HTML)

I. Title.

PS8576.A5494B33 2017   C813'.54   C2017-904540-7
C2017-904541-5

Cover design: angeljohnguerra.com
Interior text design: Tannice Goddard, bookstopress.com
Printer: Friesens

Printed and bound in Canada.

CORMORANT BOOKS INC.
10 ST. MARY STREET, SUITE 615, TORONTO, ONTARIO, M4Y 1P9
www.cormorantbooks.com

To Drum and Luke
My life's silver linings

"I heard them cry — the peacocks.
Was it a cry against the twilight
Or against the leaves themselves
Turning in the wind …"

— WALLACE STEVENS, "DOMINATION OF BLACK"

LETHE ෙ

The thing about Peacock Island is this: it happened in a gasp. And I can never be sure. I can never be sure of any of it.

Peacock Island. The memory rises out of the past, but probably not as I knew it or realized what I knew at the time. The tiny island lies somewhere in the Eastern Caribbean. Even today I have no idea exactly where, nor how Daniel found it. I like to think he was sailing through the Windward (or was it the Leeward Islands?) and, plunging and swaying, came upon land seeking shelter from dark, desperate skies and the unleashed waters of a dangerous storm; or maybe he happened upon this place by chance — a romantic weekend sailing, saw it against the glistening of water in sun, a knuckle of green, dense and mysterious, drawing his endless curiosity to a hospitable dock where he dropped anchor.

This was not an island with the promise of beach and palms. This was the menace of steep rock coast, guarded by a moat deeply blue, the tiny island rising with huge, dark trees, ferocious, jagged iguana tails in day-old western light.

There he wanted to write his book on Columbus.

"I am a sailor," he declared. "I can write that book."

ෙ

After University, after his broken marriage, armed with his Commonwealth poetry prize, he had spent five years travelling through the United States and Europe on various long fellowships and shorter writers' residencies at colonies or retreats. He went to academic centres in Italy and France. He was guest lecturer at semi-prestigious universities. His letters to me at the time reflected a strange disembodiment of the man I had known as mind and flesh, ideas and words, when as students we knew we would live forever. Now he was flying in those big silver bellies he had once described in a youthful poem as "quivering," coming to Jamaica from Trinidad, to our university at Mona, from his island to mine, for the first time. I would try to imagine him struggling through airports with his battered old bags and typewriter case, or sitting writing at a desk in a window looking over some hillside vineyard through his crookedly seated, greasy black-framed glasses, or maybe from a Montana ranch watching maverick horses canter measuredly over the evergreen — or would they be snowy? — fields of distance, calculating their freedom behind tidy white wooden paling. I'd still see his occasional article in Caribbean newspapers that he clipped and addressed to me, his writing now obsessed with foreign politics, intricate and stealthy, woven cobwebs, proof of continuing life from some abandoned, untended room of his life.

And then he had abruptly ended the exploration of his exile and went home. Home to the islands.

To an islander, any island can become home.

"I cannot write for the world anymore," he told me. "Time is running out. I must now shed the world and write only for myself."

That was Daniel. His drumroll didn't startle me. He had always had that sense of urgency, as though he could hear time's heels slapping the pavement behind him. I never understood it, for me, time seemed to be in abundance. Although I'd played the role of tragic heroine in my youth, I always lived with the instinct that I must witness and grieve. My fear was that I would outlive all whom I knew.

This place had all the myth of exile, of adventure and desert-island simplicity. It had a mysterious otherness, one that one sensed could not be defined by predictable assumptions.

Peacock Island spoke of an epic quest that Columbus would applaud. Daniel couldn't resist the challenge as he too was launched on his own fearful adventure — writing the novel that would engage all of him — that gathered up and ordered all that he'd been, known, rejoiced in, suffered.

"I understand the sea. I understand Columbus," he said.

The island was somewhere off St. Vincent; that's the airport I flew in to. I wanted Daniel to meet me there, but he was adamant: if he ever left, he'd never go back. He spoke to me, he said, from a radio phone; the only one on the island, it belonged to the local coast guard. He sounded as if he were standing in heavy rain. He needed me, he said. I needed him more, but before I could tell him, the line went dead.

The boatman would fetch me and bring me over, he'd said. And he did. As promised, a silent, stocky half-Indian dugla youth with the lightest brown eyes — almost yellow — met me wordlessly with a piece of cardboard bearing my name in Daniel's almost pretty handwriting. It was frilled like decorative grille work, too coy for the usual severity of his thoughts. When we got to the dock, the boatman pointed to a small, flat-bottomed ferry already heavily loaded with boxes. I worried it sat too low in the water. He pulled one end toward the two of us with the rope, and helped me climb over the side, pointing to a small bench at the bow. I balanced myself, taking my unsteady seat. I thanked him as he dropped the old grey bag down beside me like a sorrow, and hurried off to detach the rope from the dock, jump on board and position himself by the motor at the stern. The vessel was now even lower in the water and, facing each other, we were now a see-saw, me up, he down.

Deep hulls soften water. This water was hard. The shallow motorboat tearing along its unyielding surface, slamming hard, a door banging over and over, shutting against comfort or hope as we tensed to prepare for the next blow. He faced our journey while I watched St. Vincent recede to a smudge, the wake of the past churned up into a keloid from which we were being propelled. I thought about the manuscript in my bag. A story about my grandfather Ernest, long dead, and steadied myself by watching the youth's face at the centre of a manic choreography of whipping locks, as though it were a fixed point of reference for a dancer's pirouette until he pointed beyond me and I turned round to the sight of land approaching. It was hard to see anything. Shading my eyes with one hand, I looked into the late afternoon sun that made the sea shine like glass. It slowly came into view in stony greys and dark green, feral and wilful, a clutter of windblown rock face and ungroomed trees turned away from welcome. A feeling of recognition overwhelmed me, as it had on the birth of my first son; I knew this face I'd never seen before, that this meeting would always be important to me.

The ferryman cut the engine to a stutter. Apart from a small dock that extended quite far out into the sea, I saw no other access to the island, not a single house from the water as we approached; only an old wall, the side of a tall building that looked like a fort with light glinting from small domed windows, with a cannon like some dinosaur bone perched at its western tip, more history than destiny.

And there he was: Daniel, standing on the dock, a speck that grew larger as we puttered in.

I remember that moment, navigating the last few feet to each other after all those years, the two of us who had gone on living our daily lives quite normally beyond one another. Now here we were again, as though we had simply got misplaced, and now, despite the vastness of the world, we'd found exactly the same small point on the map. Us.

"What a thing!" he said as the boy jumped over the edge to moor the boat. I stood, reaching out for balance to take Daniel's outstretched hands, one of which he retrieved for a moment to toss away the habitual cigarette smoldering from his lips.

I had no idea where I was, but I knew at the time I was committing this scene to the unbearable beauty of memory.

He helped me over the side with my small, dense bag. Because of its importance to me, I insisted on carrying it myself. For a moment, it was clutched between our bellies as he leaned down to embrace me, his head resting for a tender moment on mine. He smelled of smoke and wood chips. This was the Daniel I knew.

"I can't find this place on a map." I really couldn't.

"I don't even know if it is on a map. I call it Peacock Island. It's got more peacocks than people. That's why I came here."

One of his eyes was drifting, always dreaming, searching for something somewhere else, while the other gazed at me. I felt self-conscious. I must have looked so much older.

"I am falling into my fault lines." It had been a decade since I'd seen him.

"Fault lines are character," he replied chivalrously.

Or our personality. Then it would become a long debate. What's the difference between character and personality? He would say character is dna. Or I would say it was fashioned by the wherewithal one has to survive. He would say personality was determined by whom one learned to communicate with early in life. I would say it was dna. Or maybe it was the other way around.

"Doesn't a story have to have an end?"

"No."

"How come?"

"Because death happens."

We always bantered. Sometimes I can't remember which thoughts were his and which were mine.

He'd smile with his closed, gently amused shuffle of the mouth, corners drawn down and tightened into one of an infinite number of choreographed little knots, each meaning something unique, each for a different person, one eye gazing intently at some point to which he'd attach his stare, the other remaining strangely detached as though dreaming, they were never quite the same. It was as though the determined acrobatics of our discussions over the years would never unbalance him. And over many years they seldom did.

I had expected him to look middle-aged, maybe paunchy and plumper. He still had a largeness about him, with soft shoulders that seemed to stoop graciously to greet me, yet he looked gaunt in a seaworthy way, his gentle brown skin maybe a shade darker, unde-fended from sun. He appeared more defined than I remembered him, now fully grey at fifty-three, his eyes had gained their majesty with pale rings around the pupils; he had intensified rather than mellowed. His face had lost its youthful puppy fat; its expressions had sculpted indents, two gutters on either side of his mouth with a single strong lengthwise frown line down the centre of his forehead. But when he smiled, the sweetness from his youth returned.

We walked up a crumbling bank of mossy stone steps onto a clear-ing amongst the trees. His familiar smoker's cough was now more of a sustained hack. At one point I almost slipped, but he grabbed my arm.

"Lethe, you still teeter!" He looked delighted.

"I'm struggling with this damn bag." But I wouldn't let go of it.

The ferryman followed us with some of the boxes he was stack-ing at the top of the stairs. I thanked him but he paid me no attention.

I asked his name.

"Charon," said Daniel.

"But that's a girl's name," I whispered.

"No, spelled with a C. The Ferryman. You should know that!"

"Don't speak so loud!"

"Charon," I called out to him again.

"He can't hear you, he's deaf."

"Oh," I said, thinking how easily two words gave an ominous journey context.

"My place is just up there, but I want to circle the island first to show you."

I worried about circling an island when I hadn't used a bathroom in hours, but he assured me it wouldn't take long.

He led me to an old convertible sports car that smelled of damp and dogs. It belonged to his neighbour, he said. So there were other people!

"The car doors don't open," Daniel explained, looking awkwardly at me as though not sure what a woman can and cannot do at fifty, and then helped me climb over the low side door before heaving his large frame over and behind the wheel. It had been so long. I sat there feeling shy.

He turned to me and nodded once, firmly, with satisfaction.

"You're here, Lethe."

The silence of this place gave not even an echo back.

And then, as with everything he did, he composed himself and turned the ignition key, pleased when it started, and we set off bouncing along the narrow, crumbling shape of road cracked like an old grave. We passed only the occasional outline of a house, no more than a suggestion of human life glimpsed between this last sanctuary of Caribbean trees, monarchs of their kingdom. All the roads were dead ends. They stopped after a mile or less, giving way to a spongy hash of leaves till the worn tires swerved and then gripped on to a new stretch of dishevelled, defeated paving.

I had never seen trees so tall. They must have been there from the beginning of time. They caused darkness, a sense of sunken under-worldliness that felt to me like a new dimension. Where before I had known a world of mountains, this was a place defined by its valleys, valleys with no mountains, valleys as the lap of trees, valleys as the only things one could access. I was seeing the place through Daniel's eyes and mind, trusting it all in the sense of nowhere else to go, like some psalm whose number we know to go to for refuge — but this place held only comfort for me. I was quite unafraid as I searched for the time of day through the glimpses of sky.

"This place is profound, no?"

Daniel always made the word profound sound more profound. Though he said it without gravitas, lifting the last syllable in Trini-dadian glee instead of giving in to it, lowering my voice in awe as I would, yet it carried a sense of applause and celebration. Trinidadians had a way of speaking as though to an audience.

"A place like this could make a person believe in the sacred," he said reaching to hold my hand for a moment.

"Or become scared. Who owns this island?" None of it made sense to me and Daniel was enjoying being mysterious.

"Aesop and the peacocks."

Aesop, the silent ferryman's father. The coast guard. The neigh-bour, he explained.

Whoever owned it originally, whatever administrative hands had wrested it from the days of its abandoned fortress, had forgotten all about it by now. Ten families lived there, as far as he knew, and he, Daniel, was their only visitor. These were old families who'd been there for generations. They leave to work and have their children, and then they return to die.

"Like an elephant graveyard?"

"Something like that. A return to one's self."

"What peacocks?" I asked.

"You will meet them."

Daniel stopped the car with the engine still running and pointed to a grey beachhead beyond huge sea grapes and almond trees. The leaves were lush and much larger than I was used to in Jamaica or Barbados.

"The only beach with sand," he said. "Battle Beach."

"Grey sand," I noted disapprovingly. We'd always argued over the colour of island sand. He liked the growl of dark sand and churning waters to fight. He was a strong swimmer. He said I was like a tourist looking for white sand and calm water.

"Why Battle Beach? What battle?" I asked. I couldn't think why colonial powers would fight for this small atoll.

"Fools like me battling the waves." He winked knowingly at me, enjoying a reference point from our common history. When we were young his quick little winks annoyed me; I must have been getting soft, for now it was just a familiar small expression, one of his punctuation marks that had become part of our shared language.

He turned the car around and we drove away.

Although I come from islands, I grew up in a city. Island cities like Kingston born of European colonial history whose imprint stands sturdy, mocking the idealism and graffiti of national will, make us feel safe somehow, not because they promise hospitals and libraries and theatres and post offices and churches; but, beyond that, they possess something I was now searching for — some sense of order imposed on the land. As we bumped along I could only think of this missing concept I had known vaguely as a hymn in my head about Jerusalem, and vowing to thee my country and paths of peace. Something that promised our lives shape and the hope of certainty.

"How on earth did you find this place?"

He ignored my question.

It was still quite light, and after more stretches of broken paving, we came to an abrupt stop in a clearing.

"Full circle," he said with satisfaction.

That's when I saw the windmill that would come to represent that strange, unresolved place and time.

And it was strange. It was something totally new, something in the middle of our years that held none of the disappointment, none of the squalidness or drudgery, the falling short and falling off, the sheer shortcoming of our living held up against the dreams of youth. Looking back, this was just a moment in time, less than a month. Sometimes I think maybe it's still there, the way I left it, the old damp windmill silently standing with motionless arms, narrow oblong holes in its massively thick stone walls, neither welcoming nor forbidding, with huge, rough double doors, two single planks of a giant tree trunk, shrugged wide open.

This may read like a bad film script, but with the memory I hear music. Ravel's Pour une enfante defunte. I tried to find out what the words meant, because they didn't make sense to me, and Daniel told me "nothing, really." He was, I thought, deliberately vague. Ravel probably just liked the sound of those words, he said. Enfante defunte. But defunte means deceased or dead. I think the infante is not enfant, child, but from the Spanish infanta, a princess. Music for some dead princess. And that music reminds me now of the trees, the deep leaves and the damp, a world locked away in time by the sea. Of Daniel as the great composer, and me his heart's dead princess.

It wasn't playing when we got there. Distance has made me sentimental, but it was nothing like that at the time. It's just got stuck in my mind because during the subsequent days Daniel kept playing the tape over and over on his small machine.

Aesop first converted the windmill into rustic accommodation for a sailor who had found the island while travelling around the

world and who wanted to return one day. He never returned. Perhaps
he died at sea. Then, for the past ten years an old man called Esopus
who came originally from the Dutch Antilles, but had spent his life
in Europe, came home to the Caribbean to study what he found
there, from fossils to genetics and, eventually, to die. And now Daniel
lived there.

There was only one farm on the island, and this had been its
windmill.

"Aesop runs the show," said Daniel.

He also had the only phone, chickens, peas, potatoes, and carrots.
He owned a few mules and several donkeys, one of three old cars
on the island — and an open-backed van, the only bulldozer and the
only tractor; the ferry that brought the necessary imports that, as
the coast guard vessel, often rescued the odd fisherman clinging
to an overturned hull. At the side of Aesop's house he ran a small
shop where the handful of islanders came for first aid or to purchase
produce from the farm, sardines or condensed milk — canned or
packaged items the silent Charon brought over on the ferry, and
whatever space was left for bread and newspapers, both of which
Daniel considered mandatory items, equally perishable.

"No man comes to Peacock Island, except by him," Daniel stated
biblically. I wasn't sure whether he meant Aesop or Charon.

A Samaans tree emerged out of the shadows. The half-light
beneath its ceiling gathered obdurate as if we faced a mountain.

As my eyes absorbed the deep under-shade that was darker than
the afternoon beyond, I saw its heavy arms sinking down over everything, and although only some of its limbs were evident at the front
of the windmill, I could tell the tree and its trunk were massive,
extending out of view. We stood beneath it in a mostly sandy clearing with remnants of concrete, with recently swept leaves stacked up
against a zinc fence that marked the boundary to Aesop's property.

And there were the peacocks. Glorious peacocks. Their folded tails draped and trailing like complicated fans of menopausal widows.

Then I saw Aesop.

There are places in the world where modernity has no sway; where nature and man seem to have at some point in time worked out a compromise. This was truly Aesop's land. His presence seemed to swirl in an elemental cloud against a haze of early moonlight, funnels streaming down, dust motes stirring in their way up. The Samaans tree was its own forest and Aesop was its faun. A wide-faced man, one eye with a milky film spread over its story, many missing teeth revealed when he laughed. He never smiled.

"Meet Lethe." Daniel presented me to Aesop like a queen, and I met him almost eye to eye as he was no taller than his son. I shook this new hand, dry and brown, essential, unaccustomed to mere pleasantry, with a firm hold that yet was on his part oddly neutral, expressing neither welcome nor weakness nor strength, more indifference or tolerance, a patience with anyone whose hand he had to shake. To belong here was a timeless business, one that would need no introduction or farewell. I felt I was shaking the island's hand.

And that's when I saw him. The magnificent bird, a peacock at least twice the size of the rest, strutted out, and, finding himself on show, performed a pompous ritual, puffing up his tail as though on the runway of some celestial theatre, the feathers on his forehead a tiny, elaborate hat bobbing up and down, just a little swagger, and then he stopped, suddenly closed down his brief show and reached for the ground to perform the simple function of pecking, his long train of now closed feathers sweeping the ground. Unlike the other peacocks he was jet black. The tallest of the birds, a splendid specimen who kept his distance from the brood, hovered near Aesop.

"See, he's welcoming you!" said Daniel, obviously pleased with what he saw as my red-carpet treatment.

Daniel was prone to hyperbole. The flattery was good for my ego.

"This is Othello," Aesop said as though formally presenting the bird who'd now turned his back and looked anywhere but at me.

"But he's black!" I exclaimed. A Nubian peacock. I'd never seen such a sight.

Neither man offered an explanation.

"So, what. You prejudiced?" He cackled. "Dan, man, you can't celebrate the lady without the fatted calf."

Aesop's earthy informality surprised me. No one I ever knew called Daniel "Dan."

He returned briefly to his neighbouring cottage, surrounded by shrubs, to re-emerge proudly gripping a plucked chicken by its twiggy feet. Othello waited at the door and as Aesop reappeared he followed his master, apparently unfazed by the corpse of a fellow fowl being held aloft.

Daniel frowned at the carcass with distaste. "Cut it up for me, nuh? I don't have a good knife. Anyway, the oven doesn't work."

Aesop sucked his teeth. "The oven work. You just need wood. Chu, is you pack it up with all you damn stuff." He walked over to the windmill, leaving his footprints in the freshly brushed sand. He went inside to sort out the oven, an old black Dover stove, which did indeed house a few provisions that Aesop promptly removed. He then fetched dry wood and soon had the old stove lit.

"Even the taciturn Aesop has fallen under your spell," mused Daniel. He sometimes used florid words in the most everyday conversation. But not for effect. It's just how he thought and spoke. "Can you roast a chicken, Lethe?"

"I will roast you a chicken." I was suddenly feeling lighter, as though this ordinary, mindless task that I had performed so often for my children would bring me peace.

"What, you've learned to cook?"

"When you have two sons to feed, believe me, you learn. But you must remove the neck and gizzard, liver — all those innards, and the parson's nose." This was no supermarket chicken.

"The pope's nose," he corrected me. Trinidadians are usually Catholic.

"Pope's, parson's, whatever."

Aesop's laugh was like a squall, sudden and wicked. "She ain't like de fowl batty!"

He felt familiar, crude and revelling; like every mountain carpenter I'd ever known. He lit the lamps that smelled of the kerosene from my youth. A windmill's arms may be long, but inside was compact, like fitting into a caravan. The walls seemed to sway precariously to the metronome of our lamp-lit walk.

The sound of the sea shook us with every wash, making even our stillness seem like a journey.

Daniel pushed open a glass-paned double doorway to a long room. Dark as we first entered, Aesop brought another lamp. I could hear the sound of the sea following us, the room being nearest the cliff, its presence felt louder pounding through the walls.

And then like magic, before even I saw them, the familiar smell of books. A world whose body exuded a pungency that I remembered as moisture and paper, the acridity and rot of mould, a lingering fragility of age and thought and memory held together in its own private ecology.

Anywhere Daniel lived, the first thing I became aware of was his books. But this was something way beyond his usual collection, which must have been stored away in some previous life. This library was huge.

Daniel watched me straining to read titles in the gloom.

"I wonder, if our writing survives down the years, will anyone connect you with Jamaica and me with Trinidad?" I thought that an odd thing to ask. I assumed only these islands would ever hear of us. No matter where I roamed, home was in me. Surely one's writing would reflect that?

"Isn't our island there in all we write, no matter where we live?" I said. "Margaret Laurence once said the place we grew up in is the person we are. You will make Columbus Trinidadian!"

I sensed his smile. I believe he liked that.

I followed him into the dim afternoon light of the room, where at the far end were two large windows, one of stained glass I'd noticed from outside. It glinted and refracted the dying light like a prism of what appeared to be the brilliant circular panes depicting a peacock's tail.

"A bright peacock!" Even in the late light I could see the aqua and green, the navy eye of each feather. I thought its presence strange and wondered what came first, the window or the flock of birds outside.

"This room is where Esopus worked. Those are just a few of the books he collected." Daniel pointed to the long walls behind and on either side lined with ceiling-high shelves stuffed with tomes, upright and sideways. There were more in stacks all over the floor.

"It's said he was the Dutch ambassador to Spain during the civil war."

Daniel had met the old man when he first came to see the place; he had heard he was leaving for the mainland. He spoke eight languages and wrote several internationally acclaimed books on music, anthropology, and cooking. While in Spain his "real" library was burned to the ground. When Daniel met him at the windmill in his last years, this was the biggest home library Daniel had ever seen — maybe ten thousand books. At age nineteen he wrote a book about peacocks that would become a seminal work on these birds.

"Black peacocks?"

"Dunno. Peacocks!"

He told Daniel he'd decided to leave Europe when he stopped going to concerts, stopped listening to classical music, and would now only read the scores. "They can never play it as perfectly as I hear it in my head," he'd said.

Daniel didn't know what had brought him to this island, this windmill overlooking the sea. Aesop was a man of few words, he said. Did he bring the peacocks? Did he install the stained-glass window?

"Ask Aesop."

Guiding me, Daniel walked over to the dark shape of a large, polished desk under the plain window, with an elaborately carved chair that in the half-light looked like a gargoyle facing the window. He placed the lamp on the desk then ran his long, tapered brown fingers, forever wrinkled as though water-logged at their tips, over the shoulder of the chair. Then he gripped it, leaning back as though at a podium and turned to address me.

"You know what he told me? Look, I've turned my desk around. Don't want to see all those books anymore. Now I only study the sea."

In his last years, the old man had been full of despair, and more than a little intolerant. But in that time he founded a little museum on the mainland, doing groundbreaking work on the Caribs or Tainos — Daniel didn't seem quite sure — who'd originally inhabited the islands.

When Daniel met him, the old man explained that his health was failing and he had to return to the mainland. Daniel agreed to rent the windmill. By the time Daniel packed up and returned, the old man had died right there at his desk. He was in his late eighties. He had not left the island.

Daniel had placed his typewriter on the desk under the plain window facing the sea. This was now his study.

I stared at the stacks. It was a labyrinth whose odour we breathed, beloved books and more books, old, leathered, papered, weathered and withering, mildewed. Yellowing books perspiring through heat and damp and time and their DDT, a smell I knew well from Ernest's library, intimate as a million tiny musky underarms, a netherworld of books. Books in some gallant last stance against time; books I discovered as I walked slowly through their ranks that someone had lovingly read and sorted and placed and framed with a sense of subject and era and theme and genre and author and occasion into shelves in formation, nestled shoulder to shoulder, tall as the thin boundaries of their spines, guarded by the closed arms of their covers, their contents a single dignified, respected life with secrets and efforts and precious births and happiness and bending sorrows tucked into their pages to sleep forever if nobody roused them by taking them down from their shelves.

We stood, as if inspecting the guard, as the phalanx of books stood at attention in formation through the cool, shadowy room that seemed to widen out and reveal itself to me. It looked as large as a small country church, and its contents climbed to the high ceiling. Books that someone had held dear, each hallowed by this its last, lost outpost of defended dignity.

He looked solemnly at me.

"When a man turns his back on his books, he's ready to die," Daniel said.

"But Daniel, you've turned your back to the books!"

"I want to face the sea, Lethe. I'm writing about Columbus."

He lifted the light to show me the deep ledge of sill behind the desk. I saw a little crowd of arranged photographs, some of which I remembered, recognizing them by their frames before making out the pictures — his dead mother, eternally young, lying on her side on a beach in Barbados, propped up on one elbow to smile at the

camera, to smile at Daniel over the motherless years that were to
follow. A stern one of his elderly father in his judge's robes. Daniel's
two joyous daughters as children in coats, boots, hats, and mittens,
standing in Green Park in London. His aunts Verrie and Gilly standing formally behind a single ornate white chair. And a very young
me — a photograph he took at university, with my hair short and my
neck so very long. On the floor, next to his desk, a horrible carved
wooden painted bird. A toucan I'd once given him. He'd scoffed at
it, regretting I hadn't brought him Mount Gay rum instead. He'd
lugged it about with him all those years.

"Aunt Gilly died," he said. He took a small brown envelope from
a thin drawer under the table and passed it to me. It bore my name
in an old lady's painstakingly neat handwriting.

Aunt Gilly was dead. I opened the worn envelope that held its
treasure — a lavender-smelling piece of crocheted lace.

"It was a while back," Daniel said so gently, with a softness he
always maintained for his aunts. Aunt Verrie had died first. I knew
Gilly would soon follow. In a fast-changing world, those two had
faithfully provided both company and context for each other. He
cupped my head in his hands and gave it an odd, loving scratch, as
though I were a cat.

❧

In the awkward but happy space designated a kitchen, I seasoned
the pale, lifeless flesh of the chicken with what Aesop brought and
what was already there — limes, salt, black pepper, scotch bonnet,
scallions, onions, and some damply solid garlic powder I dug out
of a bottle and shoved inside the cavity with stale bread soaked in
some beer I found open in the small icebox that had no ice. As I
prepared the bird, I was balanced by each tiny, mindless act, each
familiar cut of a knife or shake of an arm, the stir of a spoon, the

turn of a tap, and the waltz of my hands round the soap and each other, the squeeze and return of a towel. There was an old rusty pan that Daniel scrubbed, in which I placed the bird surrounded by a pool of water. Since there was no tinfoil, after half an hour, when the pyramid of bird was brown, I covered it with two badly chipped enamel plates and left it to its fate in the unregulated blaze.

Daniel fixed us rum and cokes and we sat together on the concrete patio at the back where he'd hung laundry as we waited for dinner; two deep wooden slatted Adirondack chairs sitting side by side as though we'd always been there, our elbows resting on the wide arms, studying the history of the sea. Daniel, as always, smoked.

The Samaans gathered the rest of the shadows and the drift of Daniel's smoke. It seemed to make him cough with his deeper inhalations.

I watched the peacocks retreat with advancing evening, dark on dark, jerking, wounded shadows dragging home the rest of their day with their closed tails. Othello was nowhere in sight.

"There is an island in Italy on the Lake Maggiore, off Stresa. It's called Isola Bella. Napoleon once slept there with Josephine. I went there with Alex," I said. "It was populated with white peacocks. Albinos. Just like these, but white — an intricate radiance of white lacy brides. That would be grooms, really. It's the male that is beautiful. I didn't know there were black peacocks ..."

Daniel didn't know there were white ones.

"Othello's the only black male. The only black peacock. The peahens look like big partridges with crowns on their head. See? We don't bother to notice them."

We finished our drinks as the wind picked up. The laundry tugged at the lines, the arms of shirts flying in various directions. Everything was new to me and yet ultimately felt the same outlined by my mourning. These tall trees, fruitless and flowerless, were a new dimension, growing without purpose, unfulfilled just as these roads that lead nowhere.

"Where do they sleep?" I asked.

"The peacocks? I will tell you in the morning." He said this like a very wise man.

"The roof of the second bedroom upstairs leaks. It rains every night. So you will have to sleep with me," he said not so matter-of-factly.

Upstairs. I can't even remember it now, twenty years later, but that is not surprising. It was always somehow above us, cerebral, elusive, more like the subconscious than memory, an attic stored away, out of reach, inaccessible but there, more safe and certain than anywhere else. A place I knew you could count on not to be exploited, preserved in layers of its own ecosystem, damp mould or powdering dust, infinitely durable in essence, imploding in its own decay, its "will be's" grimly yet sedately and infinitely patiently and exactly and truly what it always was.

"Oh well," I said matter-of-factly.

Spoken or unspoken, the bedroom of our life was the conundrum — where I should sleep. It always had been, and the fact I would share his room now wasn't going to solve any aspect of our complicated relationship.

"To Jacob," he said, rattling the ice in his drink as he lifted it for a toast. "My nemesis. The man who keeps us apart."

He was always jealous of my father.

I thought of the news I couldn't bear to share.

"I finished the book," I said.

"Did you bring it?"

I said I'd give it to him tomorrow.

I couldn't tell if he was looking at me beyond his lantern as we spoke, or staring blindly at a floor plan of my face he knew by heart.

My eyes were always better than his, but now the light played tricks. The kitchen radiated strobes of light from the excitable glow of a humming Tilley Lamp Aesop had hung from a hook. The smell of the roasting bird in the oven reminded me to feel hunger.

Now all the peacocks were gone.

He smoked again. And again. I saw how sad Daniel looked in repose, how much older. His mouth, now grown closed, gave away his concentration; it was as if his lips settled around and contained his thoughts. It was still a sexy mouth, withdrawn and intimate,

"Have I changed?" As I asked, I tried to relax my wrinkled forehead as though he could see my face in the gloom.

"What, fallen into your fault lines?" We both laughed.

"Do you know why I came here?"

"Because I asked you to!" he said.

Because Jacob's dead, I thought, but I didn't say.

There was no way to know the heat of the oven, so it was just a waiting game to see what happened to the evening's meal or the world without Jacob.

Jacob's dead. If I said it out loud, the words, as they say, would become flesh. We would become Daniel and Lethe in a world where Jacob was dead, words that would go on repeating themselves between us forever. There would be no reprieve, just as there had been none in the world where Jacob wasn't dead.

I was sorry about Aunty Gilly. He would be sorry about Jacob.

We were full of sorrows.

"We were always orphans," he said and reached for my hand across the chairs. "I know about Jacob."

We sat holding the dark of a world without Gilly or Verrie. Without Jacob.

"Yes, my love, you've changed. The Lethe I knew smoked and she couldn't roast a chicken."

DANIEL ◎

I first saw her from water. It was 1968. She teetered across my morning in high-heeled sandals that made her seem taller than she turned out to be. A childlike, almost androgynous figure, pale yet clearly a local islander. I don't know how I knew that, but it was something that one knew as one looked at her. She was very thin with comparatively long legs and a cheerful yellow bikini. She had a very small face and wore a lot of black eye makeup which against her pale skin made her face seem haunted. She held her lit cigarette like a pro. No sign of a book. She was with a soulless white Czech-Jamaican who swam for Seacole, the woman's hall. I knew her. Her name was Blanca and I knew she liked me. Maybe this woman was Czech too. But maybe not, for then the stranger circumvented the pool with caution as though afraid of water. Unlike most foreigners in the islands who consider the water a plaything, many islanders are afraid. That was the telltale clue. Unsteady, unworldly; vulnerable. Ill at ease. That was my first impression.

Who were they to disturb this usually tranquil time? This was my pool before lunch. Before it began to get busy on weekdays. I would do my laps and finish reading Ibsen or Fielding, whoever, before my eleven o'clock class. But then this awkward mystery strayed into sight and I was fascinated and annoyed at the same time.

"Meet Lethe," Blanca called out.

What a name. *Lethe*. Lethe was studying English honours, as was I, Blanca explained, joining me in the water. A science student, she had little understanding of the significance of that course designed to offer nothing but English literature, from Beowulf and Chaucer, on to Shakespeare and the Elizabethans, the Romantics, all the way to T.S. Eliot, with a single Caribbean course and one optional American one, and of course linguistics and philology. There were no general arts subjects thrown in for good measure — no respite of simple social science — and it was certain that to embark on this course one had to be serious about either teaching literature or writing it.

I pulled myself up out of the pool. The Lethe woman had spread a towel and laid down and was now making herself comfortable like some damn tourist. Nothing in hand to read, she oiled herself and crooked her knees, one hand shielding her eyes, the other feeding herself with the cigarette the smoke of which she inhaled and held on to, awkwardly lifting her sharp shoulders, which slumped a few moments later as she exhaled.

As I approached, I splashed her quite deliberately. Startled, she sat up, holding her cigarette high, anxious it not get wet. A tiny face, pretty but perplexed, remaining perplexed as she gazed at me, her large, deep-sunken dark eyes un-flirtatious and still, something constantly jittery and defensive about the rest of her, making me feel as though she expected me to approach her with a problem — Where is your pool pass? These chairs are for rent. Hand me all your money. No yellow bikinis in this pool.

"Why are you taking English special honours?"

She pointedly wiped the water off her face and neck, then shrugged. "It's the only thing I love," she answered in an unmistakable Jamaican accent. She didn't miss a beat, and stuffed in her mouth a white ball that looked like cotton wool that she'd pulled from her bag.

And that was it. That was her only answer. I had never heard another English honours student give it. They would just study the literary masters, great and small, eking out their opinions like little reviewers, clucking and frowning and agreeing or disagreeing. Most of them would never write a line or have an original thought in their lives. Some would go on to predictable careers as teachers, hoteliers, bankers, far removed from their special honours degree; others became drug dealers, brothel owners, addicts, or aging hippies. Steele and Addison, Chaucer or Beowulf, Shakespeare or Walcott, the Seafarer, all buried inside them, a rare meal they once ate, a costume worn once at carnival. They were wasting time wading through pages excruciatingly created by another life. And here was this Lethe who claimed that English literature was all she loved.

And she was Jamaican.

"What's that you're eating?" I asked her. "Cotton candy?"

"Marshmallows." She chewed out the words, retrieving the bag to offer me one.

"No. But I'll have a cigarette."

Now she fished inside her emaciated cloth bag to pull out a pack. It was a menthol cigarette — which I detest to this day — but I thanked her, lit it anyway, and left her in peace.

I didn't speak to her again that day, leaving her to contemplate the sun as she alternately ate her marshmallows or smoked, later pulling out some sort of wire puzzle that she played, very frustrated by not being able to solve whatever mystery it held. But like Tristan, I'd been struck. I looked for her everywhere on campus, between classes, on the pathways, at the pool each day, at the student's union at night. I contrived to bump into her and talk to her some more. If all she loved was English, why did she not carry a book? What did she like to read? Why didn't she swim? Did she have a boyfriend? But I couldn't find her for days. I thought of asking

Blanca, but instinct told me not to show my hand to that woman.

Then a week later there she was — Lethe — flat on her back at the bottom of the stairs outside of Shakespeare class. I have no idea why a concerned student chose me to call for help. Lethe was ghostly pale, her miniskirt pulled up almost to her waist, revealing a most unattractive pair of grey panties. Her classmates fell back, recognizing me as her shining knight of rescue. At first her eyes opened, the whites showing hideously, but soon her lids fluttered and she returned perplexed from whatever catatonic moment had taken possession of her.

She tugged modestly at her skirt, even before she asked what happened or where she was or who I was. I bent over her and answered these questions instead. Lethe, it's Daniel, you fell. She'd fainted, she said. Did she hit her head? No, her back. I asked her if she felt she could get up but she remained distracted by her skirt. Your skirt is fine, I said, and offered to take her to the nearby university hospital. She looked uncertain, and I knew at once that that was exactly what I had to do, it was part of some cosmic consciousness granted me, a world of ours in which I now had a role. I lifted her as gently as I could into my arms — good thing she was light — politely sidestepping an anxious lecturer offering his car and the circle of solicitous students, one of whom kept trying to take her pulse.

I strode across that parking lot with Lethe in my arms in the morning sun — I was Tristan carrying Iseult. It was my proudest moment. I placed my precious sprite in the back seat of the lecturer's car, and joined him in the front. She was now holding the side of her waist, complaining repeatedly that her back hurt.

Armed with marshmallows, I visited her each day they kept her in hospital, which they said might be as long as a week. She had slipped a disc and they strung her with weights on traction. She was a piteous sight and a bad patient. She whined and complained, clinging on to the arms of every nurse who came to check on her, begging to be taken off what she called "the rack."

They had to stretch the spine so the disc could heal, they explained. When the inflammation was better and the swelling went down the disc would return to nestle between the vertebrae. But she would have pain for a while, and she would have to do physiotherapy.

Lethe looked at me pleadingly, and when I agreed with them she demanded a puff of cigarette and turned away, sullen.

Her face looked much younger freed of all her eye makeup. I realized her dark eyes were actually hazel.

After two days I arrived to find her sitting on the side of her bed, the contraption dismantled. Ah. My saviour is here, she declared and my heart skipped. But then she thanked me for the bag of sweets which was now opened on the small table beside the bed, lying beside a book on horoscopes. Why was she up so soon? It was long enough, she said. I never knew whether they got tired of her complaining or if it was in fact sufficient time. She was again holding her waist with the right hand, her face looking exhausted from pain. She was on a steady dose of codeine and complained that it had constipated her. Normally repelled by such an intimacy, from her it just came as though from an uncomfortable child, as she proceeded to tell me how before the accident she'd left the *Hamlet* class, how unlucky the play *Hamlet* was. I couldn't help imagining her floating down those stairs, a doomed Ophelia. I brought her prunes the next day from the commissary, boiled gently and stored in an old marmalade jar. She seemed pleased when I presented the bottle, and sat there forking them out one by one with her fingers, wiping the juice off her chin with her hospital gown. Her face returned to its familiar perplexed anxiety and when I saw her limping from the bathroom, she shared with me that her right leg at the back had an excruciating pain shooting down from her spine when she moved.

"The sciatic nerve," she explained.

I didn't know you were a writer, she said to me another day, when I arrived in time to walk beside her as she again limped up and down the corridor. How do you know I write, I asked, flattered. Although I intended to be a writer, I had never been called one before. She had seen my poem in the university magazine. She was mesmerized by the idea of a plane as a quivering body one entered. She had been thinking about that image since she read it, she said; that it had replaced her facile image of it as steely, inanimate, insensitive, and solid.

"I left England when I was only two months old in a plane with my father."

I shrugged. I told her I never had a mother.

"Everyone has to have a mother." She threw back her head and laughed inappropriately, reminding me again of a child. "Mine died," she added reaching for a cigarette in my shirt pocket. I lit it for her and one for myself.

"Well mine died too." I nearly added at birth, but turned away instead so as not to blow the smoke in her face. She never asked what I meant.

"Who named you Lethe?"

"My father. After the river. Hoping to wipe out sad memories, I guess. His or maybe mine."

She returned to her room and I helped her back onto the bed.

"Why do they make hospital beds so high?" she groaned.

"For the nurses! To save *their* backs!"

I write too, she said. Poems. I believed her, assuming she probably kept a girly diary with little ditties, drawn hearts or suns, flowers strewn at odd moments between romantically childlike lines with simplistic rhymes. And yet "Lethe writes poems" sounded like a big concept. How could a woman named Lethe have smiley suns and doodled hearts? It was the first time I wondered if her name suited her. It was a hushed, reticent name, muted, a name of such natural shadows; a joyless, fibrous, foggy name more cobwebs than edge or shining. But here I was with this rather fragile young woman called Lethe, eighteen years old, she said, with a lot of long wavy hair all tousled, and not a scrap of makeup or sun on her cheeks, tired from pain and limping around, who said she wrote poems.

Let me see some, I said. She shrugged. Maybe.

That night I wrote a short verse for her. Perhaps a little trite, maybe not worthy of her or me, but it expressed so simply what I wanted to say. I took it with me the next day and thought that I'd decide whether to give it to her or not. Probably not. When I got there she was asleep, her arm thrown over a stuffed toy — nose to nose with an old threadbare polar bear showing a grey-and-black-striped button eye; I hadn't noticed it before. I stayed a while, peaceful, watching her sleep. Her face looked so young and untroubled. I left the poem beside the bear on her pillow.

> *If suddenly you call my name,*
> *Even from the shores of sleep,*
> *Things would be themselves again,*
> *Sun would be sun, rain would be rain.*

The next day when I went to visit her, she and my poem were gone.

LETHE ⊙

I woke that first morning to screams. Not a single long scream, not a short, sharp one; it was a series of hideous single screams, a raucous round, one after the other.

Daniel was standing at the door, smiling. He'd brought me coffee. I had insisted on staying in the flooded room so he had wrapped plastic over my mattress and it crackled all night.

I reached for the cup as naturally as a yawn at daybreak, when he beckoned me toward the noise through the window with its deep sill.

"That's their home." The Samaans tree. The peacocks returned to it at night, though we would never see them. They just slink away in late afternoon shadow.

"They fly up there; each one has its place on a limb." The screams became more intermittent.

In the delicate dawn, everything looked young. I stared at the peacocks, imagining each one falling separately with its own soft thud, at first dark bundles that unfolded quickly as though brushing themselves off and taking their standing shape. Now they were strutting across the yard looking initially offended till they recomposed their dignity, the female's much tinier coronet feathers standing abruptly on end, bobbing with their heads.

"How do you know if you don't see them?"

"Oh, I know."

He told me they each had an inner clock, never waking exactly at the same time. The screams are a sequence — like labour pains, fast ones, one after the other. Each scream a separate bird.

"It's not when they wake that they fall to the ground. It is the fall that wakes them. That's when they scream. As they hit the ground."

They were able to balance in the dark, but he thought dawn unsettled their inner equilibrium so they'd topple off the limb.

"Each bird: one fall, one awful scream, morning after morning. Have you ever heard anything like it?"

I had not.

I don't know why, but it made me think of us. A preemptive cry from orphans. In the subtle symbolism of nature, a promise of all the deaths to come.

"Maybe each one wakes the next?"

"So, who goes first?"

I shrugged. "So, where is Othello?"

"He's usually first down and goes straight off to find Aesop. He thinks he's human. He waits for Aesop and follows him everywhere. They're great friends."

He'd answered my question.

We leaned close together on the deep, cool ledge of the windowsill.

"You know, they are revered for wonderful human qualities. Symbols of integrity and beauty. Through the years they have carried a mythical reputation for nobility and holiness, for watching, guiding, and protecting."

"Where did the myth begin?"

"Who knows for sure? Probably Greek or Roman. Hera is said to have created the peacock from Argus, whose hundred eyes are the stars of heaven. In Babylon and Persia the bird is the guardian of royalty, it's carved on their thrones. I like to think of them waking each day as the modern-day phoenix."

What a burden of history. Poor birds, I thought.

I retrieved my manuscript and a bracelet of brown rosewood beads from the bag and handed them to Daniel. He held the manuscript as though judging its weight without a scale, then flipped to the back page.

"Four hundred and eighteen pages. Hmm." He looked pleasantly surprised. "The End. All in upper case. How quaint!"

The bracelet he looked at uncertainly.

"That's a mala. It's Buddhist."

"A mala?"

"You can use it to meditate. It's like a rosary. Count the breaths with each bead. Start at ten and go backwards."

He smiled indulgently and slipped it on his hand and left to make my eggs.

I pulled back a bit from the window so as to watch the birds, myself invisible, like a Maltese widow peering from behind curtains. Their squawks were still frantic and ungainly and I didn't want to embarrass them further. It made me think how involuntary life is; this thing all creatures accept so meekly, suddenly seemed like the rape of gods. Every renewal. Every morning. All of us hostages. These birds protesting, being thrown back into the ring. Terrifying and beautiful. Each one a phoenix.

Were we all like peacocks sleeping on a limb of some tree of life, waiting to fall and wake? Maybe Jacob had taken the highest limb that night, knowing the fall would be too great to survive.

Did writers not end a story with "The End" anymore?

I watched for a while through the window, and fast as the onslaught of their uproar had come, the din ended.

DANIEL ⊚

I asked my friend Henny over and over to look out for the girl in
Seacole Hall. Lethe. Henny chupsed her customary chupse and said
it was all my imagination. No Lethe Strong in Seacole. There was
a room over the porter's lodge with the name Lethe Strong, but no
one was ever there. Not even the porter seemed to know who she was.

"What happen to you? You in love?"

She laughed her gentle, charming, tentative giggle, all velvet
and unexpected in such a huge and definite woman. A woman
with such a searching intellect and strenuously held and certainly
expressed opinions. She and Timmy, my two university cohorts,
scolded me for this lately held obsession. I tried to explain it was
not an obsession, but a new reality I found myself being drawn
into, not against my will, mark you, more despite my will. Something
imperious from the universe. I'd see her face in my mind, eke out a
little more of its memory every time, assembling only one frown,
one jerk of the chin, one glance or a single perplexed expression at
a time, even though by now I had seen her face much more than
once. Every time I'd see her, I got the impression she'd changed.
She'd seem completely different, not to look at — I had got used
to her with her panda eyes — but something in her mood which
seemed to drift and reform like clouds.

She must be related to the strong Strongs, decided Henny.

Who were the strong Strongs? A Jamaican name I hadn't heard.

Timmy laughed. Maybe she is a weak Strong.

Timmy was a romantic. Timmy wanted to take his medical knowledge and cure the world, little village by little village, the frailty of old people, the helpless young, unstable teenagers. He knew all the nooks and crannies, the secrets of this medicine and that medicine. He was Chinese and knew about herbal remedies, he wasn't Indian but knew about those too. He knew country people in Jamaica applied cobwebs to cuts and that it worked because cobwebs had sulfur. He knew about fever grass and Cerasee tea. He was working on a theory that the good weed from Solomon's Tree, if used wisely, was sure to cure something in the nervous system but he hadn't figured out how or what it was yet.

Timmy was as tall and slim as Henny was short and large. Our shadows — walking round Ring Road circling the campus buildings, Henny and Timmy flanking me — were predictably different at any time of day. We had been going round and round the same arguments, discussing Timmy's rainbow of hopeful solutions against an ominous backdrop of Henny's dire predictions, mostly political, about the third world. It was too full, it was too selfish, it was too poor, it was too capitalist, it was too prone to religion, it was too dry, it was too hot, it was too homophobic and bigoted. As she doomed our world, he cured it. I got both my physical and mental exercise circling Ring Road.

Henny said the Strongs were a prominent liberal family on the island. Ernest Strong was a retired headmaster who was once suspended for teaching socialism in his history class. "The wife's an *actress,*" she said dismissively. *"British."* I wasn't certain what offended her, her acting or being British.

Nora Strong taught drama and had started a small repertory company on the island that encouraged local playwrights and staged Jamaican plays all over the country.

Henny said Ernest had greatly frustrated the boards of the schools he headed, boards that wanted to replicate the English public-school-system attitudes, clones that believed in the great enabler of the fine art of masterly bullying, the cane. Ernest Strong never allowed the use of the cane. And it was known that he often added Caribbean history to the curriculum, replacing the Tudors and Stuarts with what he considered more relevant regional heroes like Toussaint L'Ouverture and Simon Bolivar, George William Gordon, Paul Bogle, and Claude McKay. He reminded us that our history began in Africa, not Westminster.

Nora had been trained in England at RADA, and had distinguished herself at Stratford as an understudy when she got a break to play a wan Ophelia to rave reviews. She never looked back, and surely would have become a significant British actress if she hadn't met Ernest, a handsome Rhodes Scholar from Jamaica.

"The end of *that* career," Henny said brutally. "She sounds damn silly when she tries to speak in a fake singsong Jamaican accent."

They had read the Webbs, she said, unrealistic dreamers who wanted to create some ideal state based on economic and social equality where everyone was politically enlightened and cultur-ally true. As if by waving a magic wand the British and all their brainwashing, their legacy of class and language, each man in his cubbyhole, each word in its correctly pronounced place, each culinary utensil placed and held according to some Victorian decree, would disappear. And in their place would be a well-integrated, uncon-fused people crossing with certainty and joy from one world and one culture to the other over a tidy bridge of national fervour. Everyone would be educated and have equal opportunity, all would pay and be paid the correct wage and know early on the morning of August third 1962 how to commence being a true Jamaican. And then she did her annoying jackass bray — hee-haw, hee-haw — heaved out in scorn when people spoke what she considered predictable crap, stating what they really wanted with their Fabian socialism was a British ideal of how Africans or their diaspora *should* live and behave. Idealism. Henny always questioned it. Whose ideals were they anyway? If you told her we needed African tribal society or chieftains in robes she would bray again and take you to task on Nkrumah's Pan Africa or Garvey's back-to-Africa message. She would bawl them out as only she could, because there was no ambiguity about *her* blackness — Timmy and I were called Custard and Milo respectively — she had skin the colour of a seal, smooth and glorious, and if any of these damn half-and-half bellyachers who carried their logs on their shoulders made a big fuss with their current fancy Black Power ideas, she'd give them a piece of her pure black mind. If anyone called her an iconoclast she'd cast that theory down as well.

I had limited knowledge of Jamaica's history or politics — of any history for that matter — still naive enough to believe that without those tools one could be a significant writer.

"Sounds good," mused Timmy on the other side, balancing, always balancing.

"Now the son! That's the one I like!" She gave a coy whistle.

Jacob Strong. He must be Lethe's father. A journalist always getting himself into the thick of things, "searching for the truth," she scoffed, smirking simultaneously. "But he's sweet on the eye."

She knew the Strongs had a house up the hills next to the university retreat. And with that she set me free to pursue my great new obsession.

I went into the Blue Mountains in search of the Strongs. Good old Henny.

LETHE ◎

"I was wrong. You're not a poet. You're a prose writer."

Daniel delivered his dire verdict.

"Now I can die. Your legacy is safe."

I must have been an unbearable houseguest. I couldn't think for a moment without the outline of pain. Beneath the early windmill mornings of tree-dappled light, the damp of misty rain, gloomy afternoons with the endless nudge of sound against the cliff, and persistent as the sloshing of water was the pain. Through Daniel's reading aloud from my manuscript, *Erehwemos*, softly, dully, sombrely like a cow regurgitating my dead, was the pain. And the pain was Jacob.

But the exquisite tails of the peacocks distracted me. Every evening these bright creatures stubbornly returned to fly up a limb of the Samaans, to repeat their humiliating ritual, never learning their lessons, their terrified shrieks reaffirming a life sentence each morning, answering some divine roll call.

Nora would have christened each one, proclaiming their names each day as if to a new world ruled by the noble Samaans, gathering them into its shade for rest, for blessing under a hovering moon left on for comfort. I was becoming my grandmother. I longed for the magic of her world.

To wake to the birds' stark cries became my new ritual —

predictable, expected, necessary — almost promising. As the clatter of pots in a kitchen augurs breakfast. It met my hunger. The terrifying sounds excited me; primal, unattractive, lewdly intimate. Uninhibited grief; a ululation. There are many voices of grief, each declined from life's language. It's not arbitrary; it can't be altered or improved or amended. It has its rules. I grieve, you grieve, she grieves. The big irrevocable. The tiny, explosive larynx of each peacock, morning after morning, left no space for negotiation with my own grief. We grieve, you grieve, they grieve. If I rose as they woke me and kept moving as they did, I could reconnoitre the day, dragging my nets of memory as they did, pulling straw with their elaborate tales.

Mumble, mumble, mumble, Daniel. "How can a turkey be unequivocal?" He chuckled as he read the manuscript.

It was Ernest's turkey. "He named him Eric after your prime minister. He always thought turkeys looked like they were wearing costumes!"

Thinking of it, Othello reminded me of Eric. Peacocks are defiant showing off their beauty, turkeys are defiant about having none.

"I don't claim to be an expert on major writers describing turkey-gobbling down the centuries. But as soon as I read it, I knew — I knew that is how a great turkey gobbles. So if it hasn't been said before, it has been said now."

"You've added a new thing to the world. Hereafter we can all leave that part alone and bend our minds to other things in the safe knowledge that it's been done, once and for always. Turkeys gobble unconditionally."

Daniel read my manuscript as though it were a ritual blessing, part of an old trust we shared. He'd once tried to tell Ernest's story; that had caused chaos. I always knew he should have waited till Nora was gone before attempting to tell her beloved husband's story.

"They are not gone yet, you know. Not till we stop carrying them.

Only then will they finally wash out to sea and there's no returning wave."

Through rum punches, which always had small flies or bits of straw floating in them, through games of chess, various stones filling in for missing pieces, he always won, through nights in the sodden room I had insisted on using — with a cold night breeze blowing in through the endlessly open porthole, sometimes with fine rain — like a mist, through the choking smoke of the mosquito destroyers and the strange glunking of the water pump, through the torrential rain when the room was once again awash — I felt my way through the dark, to crawl into his bed, into his haphazard nest, his arm, heavy from sleep, enfolding me, his face against my ear, my body oddly reassured by the moderate outgrowth of hair on his chest, I saw the moon, heard the peacocks, felt the pain. That's how I remember it.

There were long, dark nights; I had never seen such textured darkness, not even in the Jamaican Blue Mountains. Lingering above the trees, no matter the cloak of clouds, was the biggest moon, like everything here, lush and overgrown. It hovered huge as a dinner plate, a flat, milky ceiling light. It was there also in the day, a distant map of suggested mystery.

It was indefatigable.

Moon echo of the flame, one of us wrote in a poem. An image of Nora. Ernest was the sun.

"Who wrote that?" I asked.

"You did." But he had repeated that line so many times that for a moment I was not sure. Rather than sunlight, in those days I was always aware of the darkness intensifying in the trees with the endless moon as though Nora was presiding over us, presiding over my delivery of Ernest's story. Or maybe we were all gathered here, the living and the dead, to mourn Jacob.

"Is the moon some obscure metaphor for grief?"

"Not so obscure. Maybe a metaphor for mystery — the unresolved. Perhaps a metaphor for us," he said.

So, he'd remember it differently.

I hadn't any idea how long to stay. This was an idea I'd followed like a path in an unknown forest. For Daniel my arrival was its own glorious conclusion and he did not mention the eventuality of my departure. He loved my being there. And I loved that he loved that. This was good enough. I had no idea there was any particular reason for his invitation.

"You edit your story, and I'll work on mine," he declared as he gave me back the worn manuscript of *Erehwemos*, which bore his comments and corrections in the hieroglyphics of a professional editor.

"Oh, Daniel," I groaned as he handed it back. He always wore down a book, soiled the pages, folded deep corners to mark his place, wrote in columns, underlined, crossed out and replaced words.

As he put it, this would be a time when all waters were running the same way.

Daniel was the reminder of my sense of original family, and here he was happily stranded in relative poverty, despite coming into his own as a writer, a journalist, and a teacher, the three worst-paid white-collar professional jobs in our region. He was a household name in the Caribbean. Everyone read his often controversial political columns — not right-wing, not left, just full of foreboding predictions which sometimes were right — or they'd try to identify people his vivid short stories were based on.

Daniel worked in the mornings, when I read and wrote letters. I couldn't bear looking at my manuscript, it was too near a conversation started with Jacob, our first real one. Perhaps the uncharacteristic objectivity of this book opened a door for Jacob and me. I was usually prisoner of my own rhetoric, having imbibed from Nora a myth about my place in the family that took on its own reality: my assumption that Jacob had abandoned me emotionally, that we didn't get along, that Ernest had no choice but to step in to father me. In truth, Jacob had probably made way for his parents to do my parenting. I see how one can do that — assume a role and keep playing at it. Daniel had done that with me too, treating me like a child or a waif. His imagining of me saved me from having to be me. Maybe everyone gets designated a role. But my book opened up a conversation between Jacob and me, and now with him gone I was the lone voice.

Not being adventurous, I went for short walks only to get as far as the rocky promontory to sit and watch the sea, that vast, enigmatic cradle. Its indifference attracted me. Othello would wander over stiffly, which meant Aesop was nearby. The bird was filled with curiosity, though he feigned indifference. A real busybody. Turning his back to me, he'd stretch out his mighty fan of feathers and, with little stick feet, he reminded me of a child hefting aloft a vast carnival costume, staggering to keep it balanced.

"Why won't you acknowledge me?" I asked him as he stood, proudly displaying his magnificence for me. "You're such a showoff! A real Trini. Look me in the eye, Othello. All right then, don't. See if I care!"

"He seeing you all now ..." said Aesop from the shadows. "But we only humans. I'm *his* human and he don't bother look at me. But he still see me."

I never stopped watching those birds, some more shades of blue than the sea. They would wander to the edge of the patio beside the house, never beyond the grass and dirt, never onto the rocks. I didn't know if it was the challenge of walking on a less predictable surface, or the sound or spray of the sea acting as a deterrent. Sometimes, when there were only a few to be seen, I'd search the limbs of the Samaans looking through the gloom for a sign of them.

I'd cluck like a chicken, gobble like a turkey, make a little sibilant endearment as one would to call a cat — I even tried whistling and click-clicking as though to a dog or a horse. No sign of them. And then one day I practised a little high cry and Othello came bounding, stopping side-on exactly in front of me, looking out to sea. I thought he wanted to be petted, but as I reached out my hand he backed off, his feathers bristled, and he marched away.

I walked around that steadfast windmill that hovered like an elderly husband of the Samaans. That tree must have been several hundred years old. The spread looked as large as a football field. Below, I found huge boulders. But upon examination, I discovered they were not stone but spheres of wood, a grain running through them like in some elaborate dining-room table. Occasionally Othello would follow, but, soon bored, he'd go looking for Aesop, whose busy garden schedule he liked to supervise.

In the often rainy afternoons, Daniel and I would take longer walks, starting out hand in hand, but quickly split when we saw something interesting or if we disagreed. He told me stories. The great wooden balls I had mistaken for boulders had once been attached to the trees. The trees had lived so long, these growths were like their warts — the cantankerous refusals of cells exhausted by age, ancient, angry mutations of arboreal menopause. The tree had sloughed them off; a thin membrane grown across the join at the trunk, cutting off their nourishment. "If you were to take a cross-section of trunk and analyze it, they would bear the same grain, same markings, same insistent fingerprint.

"Like cancer?" I asked.

"More like DNA," he suggested. "Some unique, inimitable pattern that over time repeats itself."

Those old tree warts, with their huge swirls, patterns that end at their centre, a small, profound moment of peace, a composition of beauty, a conclusion or arrival. We sat among them as though we'd found an arboreal Stonehenge.

"When Jacob was dying I discovered I have a brother."

"Huh," replied Daniel, not as though he hadn't heard me, more like a *fancy that, then* sort of "huh."

"Edgar. He asked to see me. He's ten years younger than me."

"What did he want? Acknowledgement?"

"Jacob's."

Daniel crossed his arms and stared at the ground thoughtfully, trying to find my point.

"I would have done something, but there wasn't time."

"Did you believe him?" Daniel poked and shuffled at the ground with his toe, as if searching for something he'd dropped there.

"Yes, I believed him. He looks exactly like Jacob. I felt faint when I saw him. He lives in Montreal. Alex took me to meet him, and when he saw him first at the rendezvous, he was so amazed at the likeness he squeezed my hand and muttered *courage*."

"Who is his mother?"

"Ethel someone. An on-air personality from home. I remember her when I was growing up. She's dead now. A married woman. Nora felt sure Jacob and she had an affair. The night she died she told Edgar about Jacob."

"Leaving you to pick up the pieces."

"Well no. Leaving Jacob to."

"That's the problem with forbidden love. I always felt Nora should have let Jacob feel free to marry again."

"Well he couldn't marry Ethel, she was married already. But yes …" I pretended to agree, but that yes was the biggest lie. I knew it was me who didn't want Jacob to bring anyone home. Nora was just backing me up, afraid of anything making me unhappy. Why didn't I want him to be happy? Well, I didn't.

"Are you shocked?"

"Not at all. Maybe I'm surprised there aren't more?" He looked at me bright with delight. At times he'd give in to a male Caribbean tendency to a sense of entitlement as though the spreading of the male seed was a God-given duty demanding no framework of responsibility.

"That's exactly why I never married you."

"Hmmm. What brought that on?"

"Anyway. He waited years to contact me. He'd heard Jacob was dying. And the funny thing was — when he knew Jacob was dead he called to ask if I'd talked to him. I told him no, he died before I could. He said he'd never forgive me."

"Offer him a DNA test."

"I did. He didn't want a lab to confirm who he was, he wanted his dad to."

"That's a tough one."

Indeed, I thought, but said "Parable of the trees," as we made our way.

Daniel startled me when he spoke the word I hadn't. "Indeed."

"I think maybe you should call him when you get back. I never had a brother. You are lucky. I have often wondered what life would have been like if I'd had a sibling to play with and grow with; to have family that I could expect to last the journey with me."

"But you're my brother."

"I know I should feel honoured, but I don't. I could never have a sister and have such incestuous thoughts."

I admired the swirls and shades that looked like a honey cake in which one stirred a spoon of molasses. Though only a round stump it was loyally imitating the grain of its mother. It was amazing to me that all through nature the new imitates the old, that it is in fact a way of expressing the same thing over again. The over and overness of all. These were not suckers of the Samaans, but they were its wooden children.

"Living is just a long corridor of echoes," said Daniel enigmatically.

"You mean the warts are echoes of the tree!"

"Something like that," he said. "But I was really thinking of Edgar. Your brother. He is an echo of Jacob; he is an echo of Nora. In a strange way he is even an echo of your mother, whose death caused Jacob to become Jacob and Nora to become Nora — the Jacob and Nora who nurtured you. As I suppose my father became who I know as my father, and my aunts who raised me the spinster mothers they were to me. I have become all their echoes. My father's stern austerity."

"And your aunts?"

"Well. I adored them. But I made pretty sure I wasn't like them. But even when we defy the echoes it's still the echoes we defy. So they still govern us."

"And what is the corridor?"

"Life. The life that proceeds from there with its outcome and truths repeating themselves bouncing from wall to wall down mile after mile."

"So what about free will?" I asked knowing we were straying into one of his deeper ruminations which I would partake in until I was lost and I'd quit. I often got lost with him. His mind was like a walk in a maze as he thought his way toward the exit and I followed.

"Free will is always dictated by the corridors — who we are, what we know, how we learned to think and feel. Values planted in us."

"What about *Tess of the D'Urbervilles*? The letter under the mat? She might think she had free will but fate interceded when she never got the letter."

And on and on we went. Was free will anything to do with fate, could free will change fate?

Could a peacock decide not to go up the Samaans at night?

"Othello. Does he have free will?"

"Hmmm. Come on now!"

We were standing flat against the trunk, protected by thick foliage.

"Why should I call him?"

"Call who?"

"Edgar!"

"Oh! To defy the echoes? To start new echoes of your own."

The rain came scuttling down through the branches again. Daniel got up and straightened his back like a stiff old man, moved from foot to foot, looking restless, hacked at his throat to clear it. He looked at me as though expecting me to follow. I stayed put.

"See? I'm no one's echo."

"That's exactly why you should call Edgar."

It never rained for long, but sometimes the fog was so thick I couldn't see more than a few feet ahead. After a squall one afternoon, the trees in heavy mist gently restoring their drenched branches, Daniel thought he saw a female figure emerge from the shelter of the Samaans, like a six o'clock bat. She must have been hidden behind the giant trunk as he pointed to a shadow moving away.

"You don't see her?" Daniel stared at the blanket of fog, looking alarmed. "She turned and looked at me! A horrible look."

I frowned. It really was mysterious, but in this thick fog nothing could be certain. What made me curious was Daniel's reaction. He looked frightened, stunned.

"Family to Aesop?" I asked.

He didn't answer. I had seen that look of fierce inquiry, of recognition, on my father's face, and was sure it reflected some irritating remnant of romantic turmoil, now evident on Daniel's.

"Another parable of the trees," I said.
"Indeed."

An image of a cloaked figure imprinted itself on my nighttime insomnia, and what I thought was the voice of the wind calling, now conjured up a wild woman knocking on the door downstairs. "Go away, go away," I'd say, or was it Daniel? I wasn't sure what was real, and the dread that some desperate shipwrecked creature had visited before, to see Daniel here or Jacob in whatever world, began to haunt me. Echoes tumbling down the passage. I wished Nora was here to interpret it all.

I'd wonder where the peacocks went when it rained; whose echo was Othello?

And then I'd fall asleep.

DANIEL ʘ

I once asked a Trinidadian student to write down what emotions she experienced in response to our mountains.

Columbus named the island after them. The Trinity.

But what emotions do they stir?

She shrugged. "I really don't think about them. They're just there!"

Any Jamaican could give a better answer about the mountains of that nation. Maybe they feel they dare not be complacent.

I had come to think that all the hope and triumph, all the possibility of glory in the Caribbean was expressed by Mother Earth in Jamaica's Blue Mountains. I am used to the lower but sharper, explosive peaks of Trinidad which, oddly, had never uplifted me. They were mountains to be climbed on foot or by car, crossed, circumvented, lived on in pomp by the rich or rustically by the poor. I'd become aware of them when they seemed to be frustrated, bracing themselves against irritating clouds or in uncompromising rain. It seemed to me they were never brooding, never contemplative.

Trinidad mountains remind me of Carnival. You can take it for granted. If you ignore it all, it will still be Carnival this year, next year, and over and over. It is a contradictory land, people of ready impatience and stubborn composure. Trinidad's approach is always skeptical, the laughter of its conclusions dismissive. It outlives its history, outwits it with sarcasm and, having stolen the best parts for its amusement, won't dwell on it. These are the peaks of our trinity as a people.

In the more westerly island of Jamaica with its earthquakes, the misleading twitch of Port Royal, a lost limb, the mountains are massive, wiser, nobler and higher, towering over the people. By nature still and distant, they offer neither foreboding nor promise. It is useless to describe their astonishing beauty as they rise from where I first saw them at Mona. See God's face and you die, they say. They are a power to believe in. I wonder if Jamaicans who brood on the despair of their history feel bound to this long vista of its witnessing.

It was in these mountains I met the finest man I ever knew. Ernest Strong.

In search of Lethe, I was confronted by her legacy.

I spent an afternoon with Ernest and Nora. I walked over from the neighbouring university house, through the adjacent valley, an English garden, planted by a British governor's wife who built this place as a retreat from the heat, now in ruins. Mine wasn't an ordinary taking of a physical walk; it was a walk through the colonial past, where lupins and marigolds pushed up resilient stalks, through the rubble of untended Jamaican time, and a few hydrangea bushes hung on doggedly, blooming through all the upheavals of history.

Walking up the hill beyond, the landscape was untamed: grass and wild lilies were overgrown, the ground covered in the pine needles. I came upon the border of the property, a low fence of barbed wire, sagging under the weight of bracken and ivy, with an old iron gate attached to posts, held closed by a wire loop. A small wooden sign, greened with moss, was painted in a curling cursive: *Erehwemos*. I figured it must be the name of the property and I frowned at its possible pronunciation. I slipped the wire loop free and let myself in, closing the gate behind me. The mist hung between the trees like cobwebs, the wind in the shadows suddenly cold. I felt shrouded in a dream.

At the brow of the hill I saw a shingled roof, but not the house beneath it. Circling an orange grove, its fruit more the colour of tangerines than ordinary yellow oranges, I impulsively picked a few. I tasted one. It was bitter. I grimaced and thought that Jamaican mountain oranges must be bad-tempered. I started down the other side of the hill when into view came the stacked wooden house, tucked into the slope. It was narrow, with two storeys, a dormer window upstairs which must have provided a vista out over the hills which descended in long strides to the city of Kingston below and beyond. Far away to the left lay Kingston Harbour and, beyond it in some mystical regression of time, Port Royal.

It's not wise to be introduced to a man whilst clasping his stolen produce, but that's how I met Ernest Strong: as a felon. He stood like Isaiah guarding his mountain. He was at the top of the stone steps of his rustic wooden home, an old man in a dark red shirt. His trousers, bunched gently on his weary leather shoes, gave evidence that he had been shortened by the weight of years. His soft, thinning grey hair was brushed straight back, forming a frill of lively curls at the base of his neck, where their steel set off his brownness. Arms akimbo, his hands clasped backwards holding either side of his waist in an indulgent, wait-and-see posture.

I stood, tentative, at the bottom of his steps.

"Your university," he said matter-of-factly. "They steal my ortaniques."

"These aren't oranges? They're sour as hell!"

He looked pleased, briefly describing the graft of oranges with tangerines.

"Hell of a mountain you have here." I was still panting.

"Indeed," he said politely, looking out over my head. "Today they are disconsolate. My wife doesn't like them anymore."

And with this, I became aware of Nora, nearly six feet tall, thin, with long silvery hair, standing in the doorway, apparently drawn by our voices. Jesus. What a presence she was. She appeared to tower over him, over me, in fact over the whole damn house, even the hill. She had very pale eyes that seemed to be reflecting their own Morse code of flickering stories. I was certain I would never really see into them.

"Come on in," she charged, beckoning to me from the folds of her cheerful purple-striped poncho, the only thing about her that felt frivolous. She was an odd mixture — aloof and magnetic. She looked as though her voice should have purred, but it didn't. Relatively thin for an actress, she threw it well, an accent neither British nor forced Jamaican, as Henny had led me to believe. She entered on cue as though by stage direction, and I have often wondered if she hadn't appeared and invited me in, if Ernest would have finished talking and left me in his garden.

Laying down my loot by a small boot-scraper, I climbed the steps to shake hands and took a seat on the narrow verandah. It was like a stage set. To the left and right of the steep garden at the corners of the house and straight in front, were three energetic junipers. The corner trees were wide, their limbs almost bouncing on the ground. The middle one, probably due to the need for these inhabitants of the house to have a view, had been pruned, its limbs starting farther up the grey trunk, stretching out to the left and right, as if on guard. And at either end of the verandah were two doors that led into darkened sections, stage left and stage right.

"Magnificent junipers," I said with genuine admiration.

Nora looked sadly at the middle one and stated that it had defiantly withstood a recent hurricane. She seemed to want to pat its trunk.

Beyond the defiant tree sloped a gentle lawn dropping farther down into a steep valley where Ernest planted coffee, and farther still in the distance lay the next hill, a flat plateau.

"Is that natural?" It looked to me as though it had been purposely flattened.

"Yes. That's the only place Ernest goes to get reception to listen to his cricket when a test match is on," Nora explained.

"Perfect house site," I suggested.

Ernest looked up with contempt and shook his head dismissively as if at a sissy hill.

"What does it do to a man's ego to live in the hills?" I asked.

"Jamaica doesn't have hills. It has mountains," he corrected me. "Men with small egos can't handle mountains. Better they live by the sea."

"I am a sea man myself." Now feeling like a sissy on two counts — oranges and mountains. If he noticed my discomfiture, he offered no apology, but this began a conversation about the sea, my love of sailing, my love of swimming. I discovered they both had been strong swimmers, in fact, Ernest had rowed at Oxford and Nora boasted she had swum the Kingston Harbour. She had grown up in Cornwall — "now that's a sea," she said, implying the Caribbean Sea was also an element for sissies.

They showed no curiosity about my presence, assuming I must be one of a steady flow of students who passed by to visit them.

I was baffled by Nora's apologies for the depleted state of the place, as if she were talking about some ruined city I was visiting as a tourist, years after its civilization had crumbled. To me, this rugged land seemed to be germinating, cocooned by time, withdrawn to gather forces for new manifestations.

"Ernest has made this return." Raising her brow pointedly, she sighed.

"It's over for me," she said softly, simply. She used her voice effectively. Ernest looked morosely at the wounded juniper. I kept my silence. Whatever inspiration this place had held for her once-hungry spirit was apparently now used up.

There was a copy of *The Sun Also Rises* on the arm of the rough, homemade wooden chair where he sat.

"You like Hemingway," I observed admiringly.

"Lord, no, it's hard work plowing through it. Ernest loves Hemingway. I think it must be easier to fuck him than to read his books."

I believe that was the only phrase that jarred me that afternoon; it was strange to hear such a stately, aristocratic woman swear like a sailor. I have found many women down the years who have difficulty with Hemingway, a man's writer for sure, but none had ever articulated this sharp insight. I considered her comment. Hemingway was an alpha male, fascinated with blood sport, and for a woman this may be baffling. His was an otherness she could better come to terms with in bed.

"Isn't it strange how he validated each place he lived: Spain, Cuba, even bloodless Florida," said Nora.

"Why bloodless?" I asked, but I thought I sensed what she meant.

"A place where Americans go to be warm. They sit inside their calm air-conditioned homes and observe that the world beyond their windows is well. That was all Key West was till it became his home."

The three of us continued, talking of land and sea, about life and men, each thought an item on a hugely important agenda of the world. Not a word was wasted, but weighed and measured in a conversation that mattered, whether broodingly and philosophically by Ernest, or seductively and symbolically by Nora. They drank gin and tonics and I sipped short rum and gingers. What an afternoon. It wasn't till I sat down to macaroni pie on the long homemade table in a small but high-ceilinged dining room under a steep shingled roof crossed by sturdy beams of wood, that I tackled the reason for my mission. I had no sense that I had bided my time, but now I had a heightened sense of purpose. Before I could think of a way to mention my siren, Nora preempted me.

"Our daughter is at the university. First year."

"Granddaughter," Ernest corrected her softly.

"I know." I felt the blood flush my cheeks. "The mysterious Lethe." They looked at each other in surprise.

"Mysterious? Why?" Ernest calmly replaced his fork and looked up at me while he chewed.

I told them I had met her, about her fall and my visits to the hospital.

"Oh yes, an awful fall ..." Nora lowered her voice to a suitable hush of tragedy. "I'd no idea that was you! Ernest, this is the kind young man ..."

So Lethe *had* mentioned me.

Nora described her granddaughter as under a lot of pressure, as if this was to explain the fall or perhaps whatever she thought I meant about her being mysterious.

"I never see her around. Is she feeling better?"

Nora looked at Ernest, but he continued eating.

"Her back's giving her trouble, but she does go to classes." I was sensing a defensiveness on Nora's part.

"I'm third year and I don't take her classes, but I haven't seen her on campus recently."

"She may look like a scatterbrain, but she is very talented. She writes poetry!"

"She told me," I said

Nora left the table, crossed the verandah, and I heard her climb the stairs. I thought how profoundly near and comforting her steps must be for Ernest in the creaks of this lonely little wooden house. She returned with a letter removed from its envelope and unfolded. She sat and proceeded to read a poem, projecting it sentimentally, making it sound heartfelt with youthful anxiety.

I took the page from her when she finished reading, looked for the phrase that had caught my attention. "On the wall of my eternities your silhouette stands like clouds on twilight …"

I read it aloud, savouring something raw and original.

"That's a hell of a line for a slip of a girl." I was surprised.

Nora looked vindicated, drew back her shoulders and straightened in her chair.

I looked at Ernest.

"Not many adjectives or adverbs. That's good," I said.

Ernest leaned across, hand extended for the page. He took it, and read through his grimy glasses. He said, "Silhouette is spelled wrong."

He placed the poem on the table in front of his wife. Artistic endeavours were rightly her domain. "She needs to edit."

Nora looked offended. He turned to me, offering an explanation.

"Lethe is bright, but she needs to be disciplined about her work. About everything." It was clear Nora would be the one to indulge her granddaughter, to let go the reins, to watch where she freely galloped.

And then I heard about him. The boyfriend.

"Her very nice young man," Nora described, with her eyebrows raised rather sadly as she neatly folded her soft white napkin, offering an explanation. He was a local football star, son of a very fine tailor, that Lethe never took part in anything extracurricular on campus. Did Nora sense or already know I was completely compelled by her enigmatic granddaughter? Any sympathy was for the victim suitor, whoever he was, and not for me, though maybe that was my mistaken hubris? I sensed Nora was used to fending off Lethe's suitors. Why was I not surprised? I knew she was a heartbreaker.

"He was here alone last weekend. He complained she has given him an ulcer." Nora laughed as though silently miming a laugh — throwing her head back with a toss, her light, mischievous eyes suddenly shining through their indeterminate light colour. "Now, really!"

"Sorry to hear that," I said.

"What?" Ernest seemed slightly hard of hearing, but I suspected his sharp mind had already figured out it wasn't the young man's ulcer I regretted.

"I am sorry to hear she's 'taken.'"

Then I don't know why I said it — I was only twenty-two and idealistic, this young girl had become my quest, and I was certain nothing would shake my determination to make Lethe mine, to be what she didn't know she deserved but deserved, to be Ernest to her Nora — but I said it. Here he was, this ancient, proud and wounded lion who would leave the world at peace only if he knew his fidgety granddaughter, writer of a rather clumsy, odd but uniquely vivid image, this kernel of Ernest's hope and Nora's promise, would be taken care of. I showed my hand, albeit after four rum and gingers, many hours of high altitude, and the rarified conversation with these unusual people, embracing the hours of Nora's fine example of high drama.

"I'm going to win her heart," I promised, as though they'd asked me to.

LETHE ◉

"Did Alex help with the book?"

I might have imagined it, a hint of jealousy. Daniel and I were in the library, and he was rifling through papers, trying to locate a crib sheet he'd made of the relevant dates of Ernest's biography, dates he'd organized for his book, dates he wanted to check for the veracity of my references now. I was giving a therapeutic daily dusting of books, therapeutic for the books and for me, working my way from the left-hand bottom corner, a task that should take me another seventeen years at the rate I was going.

"Of course. He's a journalist. He knocked it into shape."

Daniel continued his rummage for dates, for notes, for anything he could find I might add or that could be of help.

I never thought about Daniel when I wrote the manuscript on Ernest.

I never thought about Alex.

I never thought about Jacob, who had just heard his diagnosis of cancer.

I worked day and night for a year, sitting for need of comfort in the white toweling housecoat Alex had given me after Nora died, and I wrote. I started as far back as the lap of youth when Ernest and Nora had stood like tall trees in my life at Erehwemos. Writing in Montreal, with the seasons passing outside my window, I grew up chapter by chapter in the changing light from autumn's calming gaze, the black squirrels' fleeting tails no more than a floater at the corner of my eye, till ambushed by winter and, against a grey wall of tethered light, I saw the neighbours' windows alight through the empty trees. I was a teenager by spring, the irreverent sun wandering into my room, snooping curiously like a visiting grandchild, me some forty years earlier. By summer in light that warmed rather than brightened, never like the indignant sun of the Caribbean, I had come full circle.

Alex brought me food. He bought me music — music I remembered from childhood on the old gramophone, Bach and Beethoven, Chopin and Shostakovich, Mahler, Bartók. The sopranos Callas and Price. Marion Anderson. Paul Robeson. The records played through the rooms of my world again. On weekends Alex would read through my work and we'd fight when he suggested changes — knowing I'd make them — and I glowed when he'd admire a turn of phrase with an exclamation mark.

I worked. From three each morning, when there was no world at all beyond my room, drinking coffee grown cold, postponing trips to the bathroom, forgetting to clean my teeth, forgetting to bathe.

I was back in Erehwemos and discovered that the dead don't die till we who must carry them die too. When I couldn't go further, I'd put my characters to bed. At night I'd believe I'd swallowed them. I had carried those mountains through many years, a small cast of characters, their stories now rushing back to me. Small things like the black bristles with their white tips on the blue Addis I'd use to brush Ernest's hair; the smell of the kerosene lamps; the brump-brump on clean linen and clothes, of small black irons wiped clean of stove ash; or the great black dog, Woe, thumping his tail on the wooden verandah as we'd pass; the tree tomatoes like oval Christmas baubles, the small, tart green apples and the bilberries; the furry roseapples, fine lace handkerchief of the fruit family. I could hear Ernest's music through the pines, and Nora at the side of the hill bellowing her lines to the phantoms of mist, her audience in the valleys below, checking the script in her hand on an intake of breath.

"If I come home and see you one more time in that damn housecoat I'm leaving."

I had just about finished my first draft when Alex said this. He was worn out with waiting. Other than his feedback on my work, I don't think I'd noticed him once for the entire year until he issued that ultimatum. He had nothing to do with the world in my mind or the world on my page. I am a child when I write, as if in creating I am owed all and owe nothing. I demand nurturing. If abandoned I will find a way to get by. I found the compulsion as binding as I did the long months of carrying my children; they were non-negotiable and unstoppable.

I was exhausted and appreciated no point of view but those of my characters and my own.

Alex and I decided to part. It was angry and awkward. I felt I had grown up and he hadn't noticed. In reliving my childhood, I had tenderly reconstructed Ernest and Nora, and settled the motherless child in me that wouldn't sleep all those years. If Alex couldn't understand that, then he couldn't understand anything.

I was impetuous and short-sighted. Maybe I hadn't grown up at all.

I called my book *Erehwemos*, packed the manuscript, cut three inches off my hair, threw away my housecoat, and returned to Jacob who was dying in Jamaica.

DANIEL ☉

There would be no easy road for me with Lethe. I tried everything in my power. When I invited her to campus fetes, she'd promise "I'll try," and I'd sit there all night nursing a single Red Stripe beer so I'd have enough money to buy her a drink or two, but she wouldn't show up. I even resorted to inviting Blanca, asking her to bring Lethe along. The omnipresent Blanca was Lethe's indomitable shadow round the Ring Road. She escorted her everywhere — the pool, the soda fountain — striding beside her like a governess, firm, lecturing, precise. She'd find a table for two, fetch Lethe her milk-shake as Lethe sat nervously picking at the cuticles of her thin, pretty fingers.

Blanca turned up alone that night, mouthing regret, but I could see the ill-concealed smirk on her thin, resilient peasant mouth. She enjoyed my disappointment and was determined to receive whatever was owed her by my invitation. I couldn't understand their relationship; why on earth were they friends? How could a granddaughter of Ernest and Nora Strong be best friends with someone who proudly declared her favourite book was Ayn Rand's *Atlas Shrugged*?

"She's brilliant. She's scientific," Lethe declared in awe.

"The difference between art and science is you don't have to know everything. Their quest is to know all, ours is to interpret the unknown." I was still young enough for these certainties.

But everything about Lethe seemed contrary and inexplicable. She was indeed the unknowable.

I invited her to movies. I'd borrow Timmy's car, clean it myself, and when I'd go to pick her up she would have invariably left campus, a note of excuse left for me at the porter's lodge. Sometimes not even that. I grew to hate that guy in his silly white uniform! She stood me up so many times it stopped hurting after a while. Lethe was Lethe. If I had told her that she wounded me, she would have wounded me more. Her excuse was usually her back. But it's not as though she was ailing up there in her Seacole bed; she was gone with her lover in his white Cortina.

I tried to get her to swim with me at the pool, saying it was good exercise for her back, but she didn't care for water, she didn't like to get her hair wet. When I suggested she wear a cap she yelled at me so loudly a couple of students turned around in the soda fountain to see if she was being attacked.

But she would walk with me on campus. We must have walked enough to cross a continent. It was my only opportunity to talk with her, to have her to myself, to sit with her when she'd sit beneath some tree to rest her back, curling up like a child against me as I sat there, pinned and uncomfortable, legs outstretched and cramping, to provide a hammock of support for my love. I think by then she'd moved on to tamarind balls, which she'd produced from a pocket. I never saw her sit and finish a meal; she preferred to carry a snack.

She was full of her stories — animals in her life — one who'd become sick and had been taken away to be put down, but miraculously found his way back home. The cow that chased her up the plum tree and stood, waiting below for a whole day. The horse who threw her when she went to ride on an obsolete race track, remembering its glory days. Her illnesses — the single kidney she said was born with, the chicken pox scar in her head that gave her fits, the appendectomy she faked. Her horoscopes. Her magic. The Ouija board that warned her each time Jacob fell in love. The straight flushes her dead mother dealt her. The calabash that hung from the wall and spun by itself when someone was going to die.

Who knew what was truth and what was imagination? I listened to them all, suspending skepticism, relishing her sense of wonder at the mystery of it all.

But not for a minute did Lethe consider me her love. I only had to introduce the word and she would back away like a cow from a gate, rise as I tried to stroke her hair, find her balance, brace her waist, and march away.

Nora saw herself in her granddaughter. She sensed the artist in Lethe. Beneath a brittle surface, I saw in Lethe a more tender, more vulnerable person — though she showed me neither tenderness nor vulnerability. Nora was a force. I had to keep her in my peripheral view so I could focus on Ernest. She was a gorgeous shrew behind a vivacious, yet enigmatically changing mask. She had the power of the accomplished, yet the yearning that reflects the endless ambition of any artist — the sense of quest. Beside her I could feel Ernest shrinking, drawing away from her limelight, from a world she would never stop conquering. This philosopher, all his thought, all he had imagined and conceived for a better world, planned, lost and grieved, cried out to be written in a book. Whatever slim essays he'd once written were left like a cryptic recipe, a ribbon of DNA imprinting only the essence of his universe of thoughts. Hopefully his wisdom was buried in the mind of some of his students. But his power had been frittered away through teaching, extemporaneous lectures and ad-libbed speeches, the notes for each a confetti of squandered moments and thoughts. He needed the universe of his mind brought back to life.

Just by the expression on her face Nora would say, "Oh dear — my poor Ernest."

"There is something unhealthy in how Nora makes a wounded thing of those she loves," I once said to Lethe on one of our many walks.

She cooed her response, "We too are her birds with broken wings."

Lethe, usually a contrarian, seemed to imbibe Nora's caricatures without question, mostly the one she created of Jacob.

I discovered there's no way of telling the story of Lethe without the reality of her father Jacob. At first I was not fully aware of him, as she seldom spoke of him and she always "went home" to Ernest and Nora, but I would discover father and daughter were stars sparking off the same source of light in the family universe, as surely connected as siblings.

Nora told me that Lethe had a difficult relationship with Jacob. Somehow I have always suspected Nora was mixed in with that. She acted as if Lethe was her daughter. She once regretfully told me she'd often suggested to Jacob that if he married and had a daughter he should "then divorce his wife and give the child to me. And look what I brought on him!"

For this was the outcome when Lethe's mother died in England. Lethe was only a few months old when Jacob returned with her to Jamaica. Nora described her granddaughter as traumatized on arrival and clinging desperately to her father, but the story doesn't make a lot of sense. Surely a baby is hardly conscious, just tired or hungry. But in life things happen, and they become the norm. The loss of a mother is a cosmic loss, but at two days or two months old the baby doesn't really know, does she? She is left at the mercy of the caregivers who make her life their work, which doesn't explain a lifetime of pain. Nora had pegged Lethe and me as damaged motherless survivors. I hoped it would work to my advantage, that she would see us as possibilities for each other's salvation.

But these were just disembodied conversations, with Nora probably feeling sorry for me. She'd fill me with small nuggets I would tuck away, until one day around at Jacob's house I saw the Strongs as a family, all together for the first time.

Jacob had fixed up a small flat with its own entrance for Ernest and Nora in the basement of his home, so they had somewhere to stay when they came to Kingston. My pretext for visiting Ernest was trying to convince him to write a memoir, or allowing me to help him write one. I admit to also going round in the hope of a plate of good food. Living under reduced circumstances, they still hired an excellent cook. Ernest's story, based on his great intellect and enormous experience, reflected his musings on the twentieth century from a Caribbean perspective, and the nascent independence movements across the British Empire since the First World War. He wasn't disinterested, but he was a tired man, and though I knew he listened, he was far from making up his mind about a book.

When I arrived that day, Lethe was there. Ernest was at a small, round dinner table near the tiny kitchenette, and Lethe was gently and firmly brushing his hair. I had never thought of Ernest as a man who would sit to have his hair brushed, and it never occurred to me that Lethe was willing to nurture anyone. My entrance had interrupted the idyllic scene. Ernest thanked her and softly pushed her off. Nora was on the patio, talking to a potter whom she introduced to me enthusiastically, hoping I'd draw Ernest out to sit with them. I opted to sit inside with Ernest and talk. Lethe roved to and fro, mostly whispering on the phone — probably to Mr. Cortina — the long cord trailing, smoking her ever-present Matterhorn cigarettes and flicking ash into a different potted plant each time she turned, acknowledging Ernest with a small wave or passing sweetness.

Lethe appeared to be one step away from the reality of what she intended, so now she seemed to be play-acting her phone call. This she'd got from Nora, a sense that life's experiences should be conceived and carefully choreographed.

While totally a part of what we said to each other, Ernest's eyes followed Lethe. I saw she was a source of happiness for him.

As the tableau settled into its own harmony, Jacob walked in. Jacob, father of my Lethe. In an instant Lethe stopped pacing and changed direction, so that she faced in upon his entry. What a transformation! Never before had I seen such utter love, such enchantment on that small face. It was lit from within. She was radiant, and for the first time beautiful. Her happiness was brighter, more remarkable than the thick black lines around her eyes; a face that must conspire with its angels and demons to locate its harmony. There it was. Utter joy. Only then did I turn and see her father.

Jacob, the man I knew to be my real competition. I had seen his picture in newspapers, but nothing prepared me for this man, at least six-foot-four, with charisma that I had never felt before. He was utterly charming, not in a crafted way, but a naturally polite and intuitively polished man whose presence rearranged the room like a magnet would shards. He too smoked. Nora fawned, Ernest withdrew, and Lethe was eager as I'd never seen her before. The potter literally disappeared, his departure receding beyond this intense circle of light.

Jacob hugged his mother and for a second I was reminded of an ex-wife holding on too long, he pulling just so slightly away. Lethe chucked the phone onto its cradle with a hasty "Call-you-back" and flew to Jacob as though she'd never hurt her back. He hugged her, gently disengaging her as he had his mother, first patting her gently to reassure her.

"Dad," he said, as he looked at Ernest, but in that "Dad" was a bond, so much patience and time exchanged between them, so much teaching and learning, so many examples set and so many subtle expressions of sympathy and understanding, kept safe from Nora's attention. I felt a fleeting moment of envy for their close relationship.

This meeting allowed me into the family circle. It was brief, as Jacob was just checking on Ernest and Nora, having to attend a meeting and then dinner. He and his father talked about a current national issue that I can't remember. Lethe hovered, trying to find an opening to ask about school or was it money or shoes or time off from classes to go somewhere. She blew smoke above his head that he kept swiping at as it circled his face, somehow hers affected him more than his own; she flirted, she cajoled, using all her wiles in that short opening to win his attention, keep him there, keep him anywhere she could pin him down. But all she got was, "Darling, we'll talk about it later," as he got up to leave.

I saw the afternoon fade from her. She followed him out. I could hear her chatting up the path behind him.

"He never has time for her." Nora shook her head sadly and looked at Ernest. Ernest seemed uncomfortable, as if he was expected to sigh and didn't. It was a telling moment, and I sensed a rift between them concerning Lethe.

On her return she was dejected Lethe again. Limping, edgy, picking her fingers, restless, distracted, disenchanted, searching for her pack cigarettes or tamarind balls.

Whoever it had been on the phone with her, she didn't call him back.

LETHE ⊙

I said, "I think Jacob killed himself." We were in the water where the rocks formed a natural cove.

Daniel did his work for the morning while I read and brooded. I hadn't the heart to tell him that was all I felt I could do, that taking this blind journey had been an act of desperate faith — my only one. I couldn't think about another plan. Now the sun had come out and Daniel convinced me to swim. We climbed down the steep steps beyond the windmill, into a pool so endlessly blue, so darkly, sleekly opaque, its intake of light folded over and over, tumbling deep and eternally wet into its unfathomable belly, its womb and tomb. It was cut off from the sea except for a small opening, and the water was placid, shifted by the nudges of each exterior wave. It wasn't as cold as I'd feared, and Daniel had lured me in by beckoning to me over and over, as Jacob had done from a wild sea when I was a child.

My mood was a bit like the water and the trees, endlessly bent on a journey that no longer had anything to do with anything but here in my head, its own sentence of memory and imagining. It was an interminable loneliness that over the years I had learned to distance myself from, but with which I was now irrevocably reunited. Perhaps that's where we all begin. And funny thing — losing Jacob was new, but I could still remember the sorrow from somewhere, as if it had always been happening, I could see it coming and see it leaving to return. It was like some dreaded relative one hopes won't come to visit.

Daniel was the part of my life that had survived. As he held me in the water I wanted to cry but was able to fight it. Tears are like a payment we make when we expect comfort or sympathy, some relief in return. What I felt had no currency of tears. We crouched there, stroking the water and treading, my arms wrapped around Daniel's huge soft shoulders, my wet hair sticking to me and him like seaweed each time we swayed, till I no longer felt solid, no longer felt responsible, and the automatic treading of water was a simple thing to do.

"Life's really all about death," he said.

"You mean it's all an allegory?"

Othello was standing guard above on the rocks, his neck jerking back and forth, looking as though he wasn't sure what to do next.

"A peahen died this morning. Aesop found it under the Samaans. I saw him dig a small grave, wrap the bird in a towel, and cradle it gently in his arms as he laid it to rest." Daniel pulled a strand of hair back from my face.

Were we all like the peacocks sleeping on a limb of the tree of life, waiting to fall and wake?

"Maybe Jacob took the highest limb that night knowing the fall would be too great for him to survive."

It was the first time I had admitted that thought out loud.

The last night when Jacob fell asleep he had been as okay as he was on any other night that month. I'd turned off the light, and sometime later I noticed the light was on again, shining under my door from across the hall. I waited and saw it turn off shortly after. It would later occur to me that from the small bedside table drawer with its pharmacy of prescriptions he could have taken anything. Perhaps he planned this all along.

"Would that be so terrible?" Daniel spoke with such sudden passion I knew I'd touched a nerve. "We mustn't be martyrs. The obscenity is pain. I have always felt it's medieval, this hanging on to be what, brave? Holy? It's gruesome vanity."

I had wanted him to live forever.

"Would you turn out the light if you knew you were waiting to die?"

"Probably not," he said, then went silent, allowing me to sort out my thoughts, holding me in the water as I reconnoitered, steering us to make sure we didn't drift to the mouth of our cave.

❦

Jacob. I lost Jacob. He gave up. He abandoned life; abandoned me. The last slow rasps of such a life counted down in six months to a gentle pneumonia nobody noticed, not even Jacob. Walking pneumonia, like a jogging partner. When it refused to get better after several antibiotics, more X-rays were done and there it was, all those years of smoking. Six months they said. They were right.

There is a rage in grief. Nothing is appropriate because death is not appropriate. Jacob's death was not appropriate, not as far as I was concerned. Nothing prepared me for what happened to him or what would happen to me. I had never considered a time without our relentless engagement, me pursuing and he resisting, me yearning and him detaching, charming but always escaping my expectations, my longings and hopes. I'd wake every morning wondering if he'd call, wondering why he hadn't, wondering what it meant if he did. This endless calculation on all but the one day of the year, my birthday, when he'd phone wherever I was and sing happy birthday in his swing low sweet chariot rumbly-tumbly baritone — so enigmatic and unclear, so baffling and elusive — but always so dear.

Until Jacob read my manuscript.

For the first time in his adult life he was virtually alone. I was staying with him, and had made up my mind I would see him through the illness. He had a girlfriend, but she kept as far away as possible from what she saw as drama. Although Jacob was hurt, he understood. Loving a man the way a man wants to be loved would be spoiled by the unattractive intimacies of illness. He could not have maintained his passion for a woman in similar circumstances. This was the rubbish I had learned not to listen to, part of a litany of excuses the romantic use for the rare coinage of being romantic. The romantic had given her his car and use of Erehwemos. I gathered she was there most of the time, often with her grown children and friends, getting on with her life.

But his comment opened up a question that had always gnawed at me.

"Why did my mother die?"

"In those days ..." His voice trailed off.

"I know. In those days mothers died in childbirth."

"No. She didn't die in childbirth, Lethe. She died a month after that."

"Died of what?"

"We never really knew. She never seemed to recover. A sort of septicemia I think."

"So why did everyone lie?"

"No one lied. No one really said anything and you never asked before."

It was true. I had always thought she died at my birth.

"Did you abandon Mummy?"

It felt so strange to say the word, as though borrowing something that didn't belong to me.

"No one abandoned anyone, nor have I ever abandoned you. But I found it hard to cope. I was young and she wasn't rallying. But you made everything worthwhile — for both of us."

"What did she call me? Lethe?"

He looked toward the ceiling as though there were prompting notes above his bed.

"Leah." He smiled at the memory. "We talked about naming you Leah. In all the confusion she hadn't christened you, and I changed it ... just a little. I love the name Lethe."

"Did she love me? Play with me?"

"Of course. She adored you."

I'm not sure why knowing this made a difference but it did. It made me feel more defined, the product of conscious purpose. They must both have seen what was coming like a train approaching. They were both so young. Maybe for the first time I was conscious of how hard it must have been for him to lose her.

Jacob asked me to go up to Erehwemos to get some of his papers. Avoiding the house with the girlfriend, I went straight into Ernest's simple mountain study, its empty glass doors staring out over the range that had inconceivably survived without him, pinewoods sighing, eucalyptus shuffling, bamboo still swaying, and I couldn't believe my eyes. There sat Ernest's desk painted in what I can only describe as a facile, silly colour, what as children we called "titty pink," one of two colours used to define the difference between a girl and a boy, as though anything so subtle yet powerful, connectedly separate, could be defined by anything so rigidly simple. The sheer tragedy of Ernest's whole life fell upon me like a pile of books from a toppled shelf. This great mind whose papers were all that was left, his ideas he had painstakingly written year after year on the simple, austere mahogany surface seemed desecrated. This icon, this symbol of care and wisdom and worth that attempted to create a vision for future generations, painted pink. I was staggered. Not just at the misunderstanding underlying this sacrilege, but that as his family we had not protected his memory.

Jacob had looked at me helplessly. "But Ernest's dead, darling. What does he care?"

Daniel didn't sympathize.

Jacob and I didn't speak for a few days, and his health declined even further.

I had been told kindly but firmly by his oncologist that he wouldn't and couldn't pull through. It was a transformative six months as this elusive figure, this man who'd haunted my life was suddenly there with me in an absolute way. I planned his meals without interference. I saw to his medicines. I nursed him as time got shorter. As selfish as it seems, I was glad to have him at last to myself.

But it wasn't the illness that brought us home. It was the book.

Each morning he would lift his eyes to greet me as if seeing me for the first time. We'd discuss what he'd read. He didn't always agree, but was open to my interpretation of a life in which he too had grown up. In a way he'd found a sister and I'd found my father. It's funny the things you can read and understand on the page that somehow never get said. In the evenings we'd eat supper together, and I'd organize friends to come by for a game of bridge.

"You really loved Ernest," he said one night, lifting off the oxygen mask after a coughing fit. He'd grown thin, down to some basic minimum needed to survive, and each frail, unsteady, trembling movement took his complete concentration.

"Yes. I understood Ernest." He'd let me understand him. I love you too I wanted to say, but we were grownups.

His shrunken arms beckoned me to hug him.

"I love you, Lethe. I'm getting to understand you too." His emaciated fingers felt like feathers.

It was said for both of us.

And the following morning the great enigma that had always compelled my psyche was gone. I had no answers. This was the handsome, proud figure to whom I belonged, my surviving parent whose life I had watched, whose interest I had envied for taking his time from me, whose squabbles with his mother over fatherly involvement I'd navigated all my life, any minute with whom had always washed away the sand prints of any previous wave on any given day, and now he was gone.

I lost some basic movement that had become my accustomed rotation; his pull had been my gravity, my axis tilted toward this distant, inspiring sun responsible for my every season. As it stopped, surely I would spin off into oblivion.

But I didn't. I just moved like a cat over ruins.

In the strange way life provides rescue and we confuse it for coincidence, Daniel called. Ten days later, after the funeral where Jacob's girlfriend had dressed for the part looking brave and long-suffering, receiving sympathy and accolades like a noble widow, I left. Numb, disbelieving, incoherent, I was on a plane out of Kingston on my way to the only safe harbour left to me — Daniel.

"He liked my book," I said.

Scaring me, Daniel lifted me out of the water and threw me out at arm's length, till he could see me without his glasses.

"But Lethe, this is not a catastrophe. It's reason to rejoice!" He was smiling, showing his teeth in a rare moment, his pleasure usually appearing very private.

"I didn't know he'd had a chance to read it. What a thing!"

His happiness now sent a ripple widening its circle across the pool.

The sun went out again, and the sky darkened pewter. Nature was there at every turn.

I left Daniel to have his swim, then climbed the bank to my

towel, which I shook to toss around my shoulders, causing Othello to reverse and flap his wings, storming off in a huff.

Though cold, I felt clearer, like a window clean. Then the rain came down like a narrative our dialogue had only temporarily managed to interrupt. It wasn't fanciful, playful, or torrential. It was like everything else in that strange place, sort of endlessly itself, soaking its way through even the thickest trees, as Daniel joined me to make our way back, I knew this was part of a rite of passage, stages of purging and dousing till I'd hardly see my own steps, till they would no longer matter.

"Have we ever walked together in the rain?"

No. I was sure we never had. I would never have chanced the rain and got my hair wet. And I couldn't help wondering how strangely things had come to pass that I should find myself orphaned on an island with only extremities of nature, a windmill, peacocks, and Daniel for company.

"Like lovers," he said embracing me under the towel as, yes, we walked back in the rain.

DANIEL ⊚

Then something glorious happened. Lethe kept a date with me. We went to the movies. *Dr. Zhivago.*

I will never know why that was the only date she kept.

I was deeply affected by the film. It reminded me of my own predicament. This film gave me hope. Maybe because she let me hold her hand. Toward the film's end I put my arm around her shoulders and she leaned against me so naturally. There in the dark across the great vastness of the Russian landscape was such a love between Zhivago and his Lara. The Russians understand longing, waiting, and tragedy. With a winter such as the one the Russians experience, one would have to learn patience. "Lara's Theme" played in my head for years after I saw it. In fact, it still does. The balalaika playing endlessly.

I remember us returning to campus later that evening in an astonishing moonlight. Its enigmatic globe watched over the dark back of those resilient mountains. I stood as witness. I was more committed to Lethe than ever. I was responsible for us despite my unrequited situation.

Lethe had watched the film with such rapt attention. I had felt her softly crying. And now she started humming as she leaned on my arm while walking to the lodge. It was the song, "Lara's Theme," going round and round in my head.

"Somewhere," I assured her as I hugged her good night, her hair smelling like flowers.

She pulled away, turning to go, then stopped, looking back at me, and smiled.

Then a strange thing happened.

"Erehwemos," she said softly, knowingly, still smiling enigmatically, and disappeared up the stairs.

That was the name of their mountain cottage. I assumed she referred to a plan to visit. Might she invite me too?

I wondered if this was her first night spent in hall.

Walking and smoking around Ring Road that night, trying to think through the dilemma in which I happily found myself, evoking every nuance of the evening to post-mortem, sifting through every word she muttered, I sensed a small clue to the puzzle in the back of my mind just out of reach.

Erehwemos.

That's when it struck me: *Erehwon*. Samuel Butler's *Nowhere*.

Erehwemos. Somewhere.

Somewhere indeed! Ernest and Nora's Camelot, their promised land. That's what Lethe breathed into the night as she turned from me all moonlight and flowers.

A cause for hope.

Somewhere!

Our song. Our sign.

LETHE ⊚

Then for the first time, waking to the bird's bedlam, the sun was already shining, not breaking through a breach in the clouds, but quite alone, a blinding orb in an endless blue sky. The landscape came alive, and what had been bleak and grey suddenly became bright, as though the blood of the world had come right back into the planet's skin.

Charon set up two chairs for me on the side of the cliff by the sea and went to get a straw mat to line the rough ground. I laid out the cushions from the chairs and spread a towel, shooing Othello, who was shuffling back and forth as ever curious at the new activity.

Daniel took a break. He brought me breakfast and drank his coffee. His sad music drifted out behind him. I had the feeling they took shifts, Aesop, Charon, and Daniel, keeping an eye on me. Maybe they also coerced Othello.

"You look just the same as the girl I met in 1968!"

"Flatterer!" I was pleased. But instantly wrapped my towel around me to sit with my morning tray of fried eggs with toast.

"How you spoil me."

"Remember that time you baked me a pie, Lethe?"

In all these years I'd never told him I merely brought him the pie. Nora had sent it for him. One of Ernest's former students had baked it for her favourite teacher.

Daniel perused the horizon from under his hand where a faraway ship glinted on the sea, the endless home of Columbus. I munched on his breakfast and he pulled on his cigarette, its glow invisible in the bright light, just a little ghost of smoke. It was the first ship I'd seen since I'd been there. He coughed, clearing his throat: *"But by her still halting course and winding, woeful way, you plainly saw that this ship that so wept with spray, still remained without comfort. She was the Rachel, weeping for her children, because they were not ..."*

Daniel loved to quote *Moby Dick* and had chastised me frequently for not reading Melville's masterpiece. The argument had gone on so long I feared that if I read it, something precious in our relationship might be lost.

"You okay out here tanning?"

"I'm fine."

On this note he left, as if leaving his island, his people, the peacocks, *Moby Dick*, and all the ocean's secrets to me.

I hadn't been conscious of how beautiful the surrounding world at Mona was before I met Daniel. It lay dormant in me like a psalm you know by heart or the Lord's Prayer you mumble thoughtlessly. Ernest and Nora had placed it in me by the things they loved and talked about, by what they honoured. They stealthily planted in me a capacity for worship.

The campus is spread across the lap of the ancestral Blue Mountains. In islands of the new world where we were all transplanted with distant, fierce histories, these high peaks towering above us are what we learn to love and honour, what the eye beseeches and to what the heart prays; they are what moves the spirit. These are our chieftains, earth matriarchs; in these beginnings are our ends, our ideologies, our footprints and imprints; our very Gods.

I knew all this intuitively. But in self-absorbed adolescence, I doubt I would have thought to celebrate any of this without Daniel.

I don't remember exactly when I met him. He says he remembers the day as clearly as the days of his children's births. Repeatedly. Until his story became implanted in my head. Until I joined his myth. Maybe it was true. It was, he claims, at the swimming pool. Now I have imagined him into my being, swimming in the pool, a dark figure slicing hugely through the water, rolling heavily from side to side, drawn by one flat arm then the other, causing an even wake which, as he turned at the wall, he disturbed to cut through again, pushing off, propelling himself halfway across the pool between laps and then sloughed through the water again. If for a moment I stood in the sunshine with the rhythm of his quiet metronome, I was quite unaware of the fact it would accompany me for the rest of my life.

I only remember that I met him at university through Blanca.

Blanca was a Czech student who lived across from me in the residence hall. She was slender and bony in a not unattractive way. Her face was all slants and planes like she was carved from a slab of stone. She wore knee-length skirts cut slyly on the bias, which made a little shivery shadow of movement that mimicked her almost invisible hips with each step thrown by her resolute, narrowly muscular calves. I knocked on her door to ask where she got her clothes. She opened it a crack, reluctant to speak to me, and even more reluctant to tell me the source of her skirts that I'd later discover her mother had sewn from bags of pig feed on their farm.

In her swimsuit Blanca stood out, having neither hips nor bottom, not even the smallest rise of a stomach. Truth is all the black power in the world couldn't make a girl appreciate a big bottom and wide hips in those days. Beneath all our newfound pride lay a history designed to favour white beauty, and with the recent culmination of all things rock and roll, and though the Queen of Soul was statu-esquely substantial, Mick Jagger and Twiggy were as thin as rakes. Beauty might be only skin deep, but it better not be too thick, too plump or too wobbly, too hefty or too anything familiar, or black wouldn't be all that beautiful. We hadn't got that far. We couldn't move that fast. My skin might be a bit washed out, but there was no question about my shape, which, though I weighed less than a hundred pounds, had a definite bottom, wide hips, and an arch in my lower back that shoved my stomach out front and my behind tilting up, so that sideways I resembled a teakettle or skinny duck. Good thing Blanca had withheld the information — a bias-cut skirt on me would have fanned out like a tutu.

Those were the days of emerging American Black conscious-ness — Black Power — which Jamaica embraced, making little distinction between our post-colonial circumstances and those of our giant neighbour, the U.S. of A. I would walk across the campus with my new white friend, more self-conscious about her colour than mine. Would students look at us as kindred pigs? I'd deliber-ately loiter a few steps behind Blanca's long stride. This wasn't my only reticence on campus. I was shy wearing a bikini, shy meeting new people, shy about anything sporty. I played no games at all. My only exercise was to ride my grandparents' horses. This was now a thing of the past, for Ernest and Nora were getting older and the horses had been sold. In this new world of social upheaval, riders of horses other than jockeys at the racetrack were oppressors, equated with the twenty-one families said to own over ninety percent of the island's resources.

My family was middle-class. Teachers and liberals, spiritual men-tors about nationalism to several Jamaican generations, irresponsibly generous, always fighting a cause, and in old age, flat broke. So I didn't deserve to be mistaken for rapacious capitalist pork.

A Guyanese student called me "ecky becky," a speckled egg, near enough white that Jamaicans would shout the familiar taunt "pork" as I passed on the road. Pork was white meat. Gone were the days when being fair-skinned gave one some kind of automatic, unde-served advantage. White was the oppressor. And "good hair" was the oppressor's crowning advantage. If you wanted to fit in on campus, you'd tousle your hair, shampoo with baking soda, and suntan. Each drop of a quadroon's black blood was precious.

"I am a mulatto," I'd told Daniel. "A quadroon. Like Lena Horne. I never want to be white. I like what I am. I'm brown. A work of translation."

"Brave words," he'd said. "But you don't need them. Any more than you need skill or courage to keep your heart beating."

I wished I'd had his certitude in those undergraduate days.

My black footballer boyfriend planned to cash in big time on my need for belonging and approval, keeping me, his mulatto girlfriend, busy on the campus selling dashikis and head scarves that he sewed from African prints in his father's tailoring establishment to an eager new Afrocentric market. But the plan backfired. Intent on becoming popular, I kept giving them away as presents.

Daniel and I had little in common. I knew that. He loved the sea, he loved sailing, he loved Carnival. I'm an indoors person who loves to play cards and bridge. I had no sport. I disliked hiking. I hated crowds and crowded places. I'm still shy of strangers.

"You're so lucky to have a hobby," I once said to him as he left to go sailing.

"You do have a hobby?" he said.

"What's that?"

"People. Your hobby is people."

Though a bond was forged through campus, through a love of English and books, through our love of Ernest and Nora, I knew there was something deeper. He was my muse, and I was his.

When I first saw a picture of Helen leaning on her car, her hair blowing in the breeze, a beach behind her, it seemed so apt. Helen. Helen could be a sailor's wife.

When I opened the manuscript, there was Daniel's careful hand-writing on the opening page:

"True sadness is actually quite lovely. Not at all like unhappiness or depression or pain or grief. That's the quality that lies behind *Erehwemos* and makes it such a lovely book: true sadness. You were inappropriately named, Lethe. You have such a dedicated, dutiful, tenacious memory."

Rubbish, I thought. "My name is completely appropriate. I am named after the river of Lethe, not the people who crossed it. The river swallows their memories and the dead are free; the river must carry their pain along."

I don't think his approval should have mattered one iota, but it always came like a benediction, a validation. As it did now. As it always would.

By the time he returned I'd fallen asleep in the sun, the sky had deepened its blue. Othello had become bored and left. Charon was sitting on an upturned pail on the rocks, fishing. I was burnt, except for my stomach, covered by the sleeping manuscript.

The sun closed its blinds again.

DANIEL ◎

The end of my youth coincided with the close of my first chapter with Lethe. There would be many more chapters; but, like all books, one is either held by the first chapter or not. And this being the first chapter, neither of us could know how many more there would be, or how tangentially and serendipitously life would write the plot for us.

This is how we left it.

There was a huge buzz on campus. A political science professor was made persona non grata when he tried to enter Jamaica. But he was Caribbean — from another island. Now the uproar wasn't so much about the fact a fellow islander had been banned, but why. His teaching was said to be left wing. I believed the first count to be a far more egregious sin committed against us as a community, and to zero in on a question of political philosophy was to partially miss the larger point, one that was impatient of debate. If the university remained — apart from the cricket team — the only truly federal institution and the short-lived federation's inspiration and vice versa, then to ban island members was no different than banning a Jamaican from coming home.

Whatever the argument raging, this was a political act by a very conservative government.

The students called a day of demonstrations. Lethe, who had never shown the least interest in politics, had never had an original thought on politics, agreeing always with whatever Ernest, Nora, or Jacob thought about an issue, suddenly decided to identify with this cause. Her reasons she explained to me excitedly, puffing intensely on her Matterhorn, spilling little chuffs out unremembered on her frenetic words, were to do with "waiting on her moment," though how any of this would translate to *her moment* was not clear to me. Blanca had tried with every negative suggestion to dissuade her — it would be hours of walking in the heat, her back painful, it's downtown and she was scared of going below Cross Roads, and most compelling of all was that there won't be a bathroom! But Lethe was going on that march, come hell or high water. It seemed to be something she needed to prove to her family. Or the students. Or herself. I wasn't sure which.

"What do you hope to achieve?" I asked her.

"I will have been counted," she said with adolescent ardour.

As though having been counted was anything Lethe had ever aspired to. I was perplexed by her burst of social conscience, and might have expected it on some cause more familiar to Lethe, maybe something related to art or culture.

Lethe could be rash. She had an admirer, a student who'd asked her to dance one night at the student's union. So as not to offend him she did, and that was that. But Alston persisted. He invited her out, she declined. According to her, he was weird and "kept hovering." Frustrated by her brusque rebuffs, he sent her an angry, heartsick letter. It was a warning painful to read. *One day your head will roll down the streets of Kingston* ... it began. A flailing, very adolescent letter signed by Alston Robbins, rejected suitor.

She posted it on the Seacole notice board for all to see. When I heard, I took it down.

It should have elicited compassion. I couldn't understand her reaction, which showed very poor judgment.

"He's creepy," she said, "He threatened me."

"And what would Ernest think of that? It was a cry from a man in love. You can't destroy a man because he loves you too much. Where is your pity, woman?"

Now again she was overreacting, trying to prove points I was sure she'd intuited incorrectly, that were counterproductive or irrelevant.

"You and I, we're not bathed in the certainties of politics or faith. We are the curious ones — that's our greatest gift — artistic freedom. Why don't you write an article in the student newspaper? That's our duty as writers."

She told me not to patronize her.

"How can I write about freedom of speech if there isn't any freedom of speech?"

She had a point.

"One has to take one's cause to the streets. One has to be prepared to lie down and die if necessary."

She'd taken to speaking in third-person jargon.

"Well I'm not going with you," Blanca told her.

"You can't go," said Lethe.

"Why not?"

"Because you're *white*. You are *European*. You can't possibly understand a cause like this. This comes to me by blood."

I must have smiled. So much for naturalization! The proud octoroon — and she was not a quadroon as she claimed, but a mere octoroon — had spoken! Blanca took my smile as support and proceeded to tell her she was being ridiculous, didn't she not know she too was considered white?

Lethe puffed up her small chest.

"You can't be serious. I am from a long line of African Strongs. You probably come from Attila the Hun."

In truth the whole argument was outright silly. I knew Lethe well enough to know that freedom of speech had little to do with her motives. I finally decided it was all part of an effort to gain the favour of what was now grandly being called "the student body." Lethe and her high-minded tone of "one has to" and "student body" with references to "oppressors" "regimes" and "movements" — and things that go bump in the night! She was reciting it all like a bloody parrot and it quite upset me to see my Lethe, who had so adamantly walked her own path no matter how wobbly, had written her own uneven lines with one or two perfect beauties, whose every thought was contradictory and though not always salient, always original, and yes, from the long line of independent-minded Jamaican Strongs — getting ready to run with the pack into a potentially dangerous situation.

But say it for Lethe, she would not be swayed.

I left Blanca and Lethe arguing at the porter's lodge, found a phone and called her father. Nora answered. Jacob wasn't there so I explained what Lethe planned to do. Nora put on her distraught voice and handed the phone to Ernest.

"What's the matter?" he asked hoarsely, clearing his throat.

I told him.

"She's going on the march."

"Well what's wrong with that?"

"But ..."

"But ..." the way he said it made me wonder how to answer him. If he didn't see anything wrong with it, what was wrong with me?

"I fear for her safety, for one thing. And I really do think she is going for all the wrong reasons."

"So what?" he said. "Do you think any of them know the right reasons or can forecast the outcome? She is young. Let her make her own commitments and her own mistakes. If it's foolish, she'll find out."

"But she'll find out the hard way."

"Well, that's usually the best way."

I suspect he was actually proud.

"That's how she'll find herself."

I hadn't thought of it like that. In many ways, Lethe was searching for something. It showed as a vagueness even in the way she walked, when she argued, grasping at straw after straw. Ernest understood her. I put myself in Ernest's shoes. A brown man who'd shrugged off racial prejudice all his life. What was his experience of finding himself? Had adversity helped him to sharpen his focus as a Jamaican? I thought of me, a mulatto, as was my father. In my island, my grandfather had been the first black man in the corridors of law. My own schooling had found me in a white school, me the first black student. I was mocked and bullied mercilessly; I still feel contempt for them. But it reinforced who I was in a very real way. Maybe Ernest was right. Lethe felt a sense of rejection at university, the current passion of black power just out of her reach. It reinforced in her a sense of what she was not. She was a mulatto, but in a roll of genetic dice she appeared so fair most people thought her white.

Of course Ernest was right. With that I took a step back, and, trusting his wisdom, prepared to return to my own life.

Which brings me to Helen.

Helen came to Jamaica to teach. She was bright and creative in a solid and practical English middle-class way, very kind to me, and over a period of months, on the occasions I allowed her into my life at close quarters she made my life calmer and gave it shape. Of all the women I met since that year on campus with Lethe whom I tried to cast out — that elusive, maddening and saddening, frustrating mirage that she was to me — this was the first with whom I developed a bond. She didn't replace Lethe, nor offer an alternative to her. It was that she understood who Lethe was without meeting her. She understood that all men who live bravely must have a Lethe somewhere in their lives. I think she also knew that Lethe would and should remain an idyllic mirage. She never felt threatened, and I was unsure how I felt about that.

I had by then become quite close to Ernest and Nora, spending a lot of time at Erehwemos helping Ernest where I could with his sporadic efforts at a memoir, usually ending up listening to music, limbing a tree or cutting firewood for him. I took Helen to meet them. After witnessing my ups and downs with Lethe, Nora seemed to be relieved to meet her. She told me in her conspiratorial way as she drew me to one side, "Helen is real." I knew it was her way of lending support, but it reinforced my sense of just how unreal Nora found her own granddaughter, or maybe she meant that Lethe could never be real for me. I'll never know exactly where she stood on that score.

But I could see Ernest liked Helen. He discovered her father was a military man whom Helen mimicked with a strident marching voice and a mimed metronome of her hand as if it held a walking stick. She'd been afraid of her rigid father. She and Ernest talked about the army, and Ernest told her amusing stories about his time in the First World War with his late brother, how before they were sent to Europe they'd wandered into an auction house and mistakenly bid on a consignment of clocks; being so heavy they had to stack them in a wheel barrow and roll them into the nearby Thames. How they once found a deserted café in France where they pinched several cases of Veuve Clicquot and proceeded to drink, finally passing out. She loved his stories.

The morning of the march, Nora called me. She was beside herself, whispering so Ernest wouldn't hear.

"I want you to look after Lethe today."

I told her I wasn't going. She'll be okay, she's tough, your granddaughter. She's a survivor. Nora said she didn't doubt Lethe was valiant, but feared she had no idea what she was getting into. "Though we are all very proud, even her father is worried. However, Ernest insists we leave her to make her own way."

So I kept my radio on and listened all morning to the news with reports of the march's progress and at about two o'clock I went down to Helen's school to borrow her sports car, which luckily had the roof on that day, and attempted to drive as near to the route as I could. There was enormous tension in town with the peripheral streets oddly quiet, police everywhere, and occasional eruptions of sound in the distance — a speech hurled through a megaphone, shouts and cheering, the wails of police cars. I finally drew quite close on a parallel street, pausing at a gas station. There was a sudden drift of fast-moving mist with everyone now running. Feeling that heart-stopping ripple of fear I heard as a frantic pattering on asphalt, I watched as they started milling around the gas station. I thought at first the mist was smoke from a fire and by instinct rolled up the car windows, but then I saw people covering their faces, and the gas station attendant holding out a water hose for eyes to be rinsed. It was tear gas. Thinking what a kindness, I suddenly saw Lethe alone, running blindly toward me. I leapt from the car and fought my way through the edges of the scattering crowd to her, grabbing her by the hand and pulling her back to the car. I shouted at the man with the hose and he turned it toward us, drenching us both as I ordered Lethe to wash her eyes with the blessed few seconds of water.

Bundling her into the car, I passed her a towel lying in the back seat to ease her severely reddened eyes. I sped off with no idea where to take her, at first considering Jacob, but with the thought of Nora seeing her in such a mess, I decided to go to my place.

Safely home, I gave her water, offered her drops to flush her eyes, and fixed her a cup of her favourite Milo. She was curled up on my uncomfortable two-seater, so I offered her my bed to sleep for the afternoon.

"Don't leave me," she pleaded. "Please don't leave."

I lay down beside her. She was shivery and scared.

"I'm a mess." As though I hadn't noticed. Her long wavy hair, spread over my pillows, reminded me of some painting I had seen and couldn't remember where, but it was so precious, so scary to me that Lethe was lying here on my bed, the very place I buried my head to sleep each night. Her legs drawn up tightly, her long feet very dirty below her jeans, I curled up behind her and held her gently, savouring every moment she allowed me.

Suddenly she held her waist and with difficulty heaved herself around and curled into my chest, burying her head and breathing hard.

"I'm a fool," she mumbled, pulling back with eyes still red, mud on her cheeks. She repeated, "I am such a fool."

I agreed. She tilted her chin to be kissed and I kissed her, ever so gently for fear she would disappear or dissolve. I felt her insistence and kissed her more deeply and held her for the first time the way a man should hold his woman, feeling her shape, being allowed into her curves and softness, the sometimes sharpness of her small bones and into the intimacy of her smell, her dusty hair, her unimaginably tender sweetness and tangy bitterness just for that one long hug.

"I love you, Lethe," said more to myself than to her as I gently twisted a lock around my fingers. The words seemed so insufficient.

"I love you too," maybe she mumbled, but I couldn't be sure.

Our first kiss.

And almost as quickly as she had demanded me, she went slack and fell asleep. Fell asleep until the sun went down and I woke her with a hot bowl of Campbell's tomato soup. She sat at my small table crouched over the cup and drank it down greedily, the way she did any drink, dying of thirst or getting it over with. Her long feet rested lovingly on mine under the table. Her faced glowed from the heat of the soup. She looked contented. As she stood I drew her to me and buried my head in her small rounded belly. It growled, she laughed and kissed my head. Off she went to shower to get ready to go.

A single afternoon had turned my life back into welcome turmoil.

When she returned to the room the glow had gone. She was tidy, but her face was tired and cold. The magic was over.

It was then I remembered Helen's picture on the bureau. Helen sitting in her car, the one I'd used to rescue Lethe.

"You okay?" But I knew she wasn't, and I knew she wouldn't ask, which was best because the coward in me didn't know how to explain, and a logical man takes umbrage at any need to do so. Lethe had her own life, I had mine. She had wanted it this way.

"Can you take me to Nora and Ernest?" she asked quietly.

I dropped her back, more in love than I have ever been in my life. But with a sense of doom. The afternoon was already confined to its own isolated hiatus, a story trapped in a book, some unfathomable, lovely poem.

Jacob's car was not there. As I watched her walk uncertainly up the circular path like a stranger, searching inefficiently under stones for the hidden key, I saw her so lonely and valiant. She finally shouted out to Nora. Ernest let her in and Nora called out to me, thanking me through the window.

I comforted myself with the fact that we were impossibly misfit. And yet, we were pieces of a puzzle to which we both belonged. In time much more would need to be assembled before we could see where we fitted in the whole.

I have relived that afternoon all my life, wondering if I missed a moment I should have seized.

LETHE ⊚

I awoke in the middle of the night certain I'd heard a voice calling. It made me think of Jacob, of women always calling him, on the phone, across rooms, through windows at night, or to the sound of some disembodied cry. But this was Daniel's home. Daniel reminded me of Jacob. His tendency to be secretive. I knew Blanca had liked him. So had Henny, though Daniel disagreed. He'd kept Helen a secret from me. I inadvertently observed him many times leaning intently into seemingly tender and intimate conversations with various girls at the soda fountain or the students' union. I once saw him on campus holding hands with an Australian girl with orangey hair. He had no idea I'd seen him. Students spoke of him as a ladies' man. Helen I discovered in a photograph. Later he'd had a brief second marriage that I would never have known of if I hadn't come home for an operation in Jamaica. I would never have trusted him as a lover. Women often tried to contact Jacob or Daniel through me. They would become enamoured after reading one of their columns and I'd be approached for an introduction. Occasionally I have unwittingly acted as a procurer for one or the other.

Was a woman calling to Daniel now? But as I waited quietly in the dark the windmill remained silent, just softly bathing in endless night rain.

I lay in bed thinking.

Henny. I was on campus one evening studying in my room, when there was a knock on my door. On opening it there she stood all sturdy, an immovable force, her eyes that strenuously avoided me now fixed on me unblinking. She'd never visited me or spoken to me before. Now she looked like a statue planted in front of me, quite unavoidable.

She took a deep breath like a soprano preparing to sing, and spoke on a single ominous breath at my direction:

"A snail impaled upon a thorn."

Then, as abruptly as she appeared, she left.

What the hell did that mean?

DANIEL ⊚

Did I mention that the student who first told me about Peacock Island was my lover? We had a stormy but at times heartwarming relationship, one that made a middle-aged man feel like a boy again — the King of the World. I got so carried away I grabbed her hand one day on campus in St. Augustine and strolled proprietorially across the lawn with not a care as to who would see us. It was total madness on my part and I received warnings from older men who could only dream of walking in my shoes.

Nabokov would have understood. She was my Lolita. That's how I felt at the time. But who she was and her circumstances as my student should have been more significant to me. But I got carried away. What became paramount was how I felt when I was with her. I suppose it was selfish in the way of some older men whose power of the hunt is fading; middle-aged men who make this grand mistake as if to rage at sunset with Dylan Thomas. At least, to my shame now, that was my rationale; the young woman, my writing student, was no older than my eldest daughter. And she went insane. Not a reckless, self-absorbed, attention-seeking craziness, but a slow, deeply disturbing slide into madness. Her mother had gone that way, she confided, perhaps a genetic weakness, a fact I discovered too late.

From the beginning Mamta was a strange girl. In many ways

she reminded me of young Lethe, a certain defiance, a gaucheness in the way she handled simple human communication. She was physically more elegant, taller, and without the awkward lilting walk; her face, though coarser, reminded me of Lethe's. It was some-thing about mulattos, the mix of black and white that sometimes left a harmony, the best of each choice, the finest possible graft. The large, deep-sunk brown eyes, the square jaw, sturdy cheekbones. Mamta was more womanly, less fey than Lethe, more exotic, and she wasn't an irritable cross-patch. She did have the one quality I remembered in Lethe: she could make a man long to be her protec-tor. A sort of helplessness that in Lethe was a paradox — the very frailty her power as a waif. In Mamta that perceived vulnerability was real — part of her slow decline that I not only witnessed, but drew me into its vortex and made me unable to think, write, or reason. I was a man struggling to save someone I could not reach in a storm who must surely drown.

Like Lethe, she was at university studying English, and, like Lethe, she wrote from time to time. Unlike Lethe, she was a poor student of literature, and, unlike Lethe, she was a mostly tedious writer, a typical undergraduate scribbler. One of her stories about a small island off St. Vincent was a description of her home.She transplanted a bit of Trinidadian folklore into its landscape and was unable to make it fit. I told her so. As a kind of revenge, she would do the oddest thing. After lovemaking, she used to leave three small stones at the foot of my tidied bed in the morning before she'd depart.

One evening I returned home to find three stones, painted black, placed in my toothbrush mug. I was less dismayed with this ominous sign, than the fact that she'd got into my flat without a key. This was disturbing.

From that point she became decidedly stranger. The university suspended me. They opened an investigation into the relationship.

I resigned and left. Mine was a cowardly act, not telling her before I left. This is how I came to Peacock Island; it was the setting for her story. Here I met Aesop, who is her father. Although I introduced myself as Mamta's friend, I did not admit his daughter had been my lover. Aesop could be inscrutable. If he suspected, it never showed. But in my guilt, Charon's silence always felt like judgment. I have often wondered if I stole Mamta's only refuge. But this is past history, a story I need never share with Lethe.

In the years that followed, I wondered what became of Mamta. When I wrote to the university they answered, which was surprising. They informed me she was no longer a student and that she'd left Trinidad. They made no mention of her next address, but in these days of greater privacy concerns I was certain that I would not be the beneficiary of such information. Then Aesop informed me she'd been in a treatment program. He did not mention where. This was about a year ago. Since then, Aesop says he hasn't heard from her. I am too afraid to keep asking, too ashamed not to.

I know it's my conscience, I am haunted by Mamta. There are times at night I think I hear someone knocking on the door downstairs, usually when it's stormy, though it could be the wind battering at the windmill's arms. I've woken up thinking I've heard a voice calling me. I listen intently, troubled as one is by night calls, hoping it's just remnants of a dream, and dreading it's Mamta. I get out of my bed and descend the stairs. But when I open the door, I never find anyone there.

The other afternoon on my walk with Lethe, it began to rain. We took shelter beneath the Samaans. When the rain stopped, and we decided to head back home, though it was foggy, I'm sure I saw a figure disappearing down the path away from the windmill. Her back was turned to us, a furtive figure swathed in heavy clothes. I didn't hear any steps crackling on leaves, no typical disturbance of the flora. Then the shape turned slightly around as if to look at me. It was over in a matter of seconds. Lethe seemed to think it was a trick of the light, shadows of the Samaans and the mist.

"It's the isolation. You're getting stir-crazy," she said.

There was something about the figure. Her hair was long and unkempt. She had a stealth, a fleeting quality. The figure was familiar — her sloping shoulders. It made me very uneasy.

This is how I came to tell Lethe about Mamta. She asked what had attracted me.

"Strangely, I think it was a story that she wrote." The title was "Mama Dlo." About a character in Trinidadian folklore I'd never heard of before. The name came from *maman de l'eau*, mother of water. She was a hideous mermaid creature, her tail ferocious as she smashed it about. Her extensive powers protected rivers, forests, and animals. Should a man trespass against nature he was doomed to marry her.

"A mythical environmentalist?"

"Something like that," I replied. "But not a goddess."

"Mama Dlo is a shape-shifter who can transform herself into a beautiful woman. She is seen singing at the water's edge at sunset, but she disappears within an infamous green flash. In Mamta's tale, a handsome sailor falls in love with her but spurns her when he discovers her true looks, and so she uses her tail to stir up a storm and he drowns."

"Do you think this illusion we've just seen in the mist is Mamta Dlo, pursuing you for revenge?"

I knew she was teasing me, but I was still uneasy about it all.

"I didn't before, but now that you've mentioned it …"

"You men are amazing. You commit a moral crime and then you invoke your own state of purgatory," Lethe said. "And a grandiose one at that."

Perhaps she was right. But the figure worried me. I was sure I had seen someone in a state of deshabille to which hopefully Mamta hadn't succumbed. Since Aesop lives here, this is her home. He is her father after all. Wouldn't he warn me to stay away from her? If she was here, had she followed me? Had Aesop told her? Why not? Did he know of the events at the university? Had she told him? I had used her name as my passport to this place. Islands nurture secrets. Islanders pass secrets. Islanders keep secrets.

I worry about Lethe. We have our own lives. Yet I don't want her to feel she has anything but the whole of my attention in this hiatus, a crucial time for her and for me. On the other hand, am I not being disingenuous? I brought Lethe here, knowing she would lose me soon; knowing how gravely her life had already been affected by grief. Would it have been worse if she'd simply heard of my death in the course of her everyday life? However I explain it to myself, I am being selfish. I needed to see Lethe. A dying man's last wish.

I console myself that expecting perfection in time spent with Lethe would mean not accepting the nature of our relationship. There is no safe harbour. We are two boats struggling in a great open sea. We are within sight of each other, but our course and survival are separate. Some of our truths are unknown to each other, anchors we must carry home alone.

That is the funny thing about Lethe and me. We have been a curious mix of star-blessed and star-crossed through the years. We are drawn to each other in times of heartbreak, loss, or danger. As though against the elements, we get thrown together for a moment to reassure one another we are still here, and then we diverge again. I said as much to her.

"A heroic couplet," she said.

Indeed. A heroic couplet.

If Lethe and I are dangerous to love, as Nora so indelicately stated, I do not believe we have ever been a danger to each other. That's when one has nothing to lose. But now we both have our children.

LETHE ꩜

"What exactly happened to Blanca?"

It's funny, but in all these years he's never asked me this before. He must have heard, assuming Nora had told him. But with his wedding and Ernest's death, the details could have got lost. We were on the promontory chatting over a drink. I have no idea what made him think of Blanca.

We had been distracted from our usual routine by news of an elderly resident of the island who'd taken ill. Aesop had rushed over to ask Daniel to assist him in collecting and getting the woman onto the ferry. She needed to get to the mainland for medical help. In his excitement, Othello was running up and down, forgetting to preen, his tail held stiffly cantilevered. Daniel helped get her on the ferry, but he wouldn't go any farther. I assured him I'd be waiting for him so he'd have to return, but he was adamant. He was not leaving the island.

After the ferry left, we sat on the steps above the dock, waiting to see what would happen next. That's when he asked about Blanca.

Nora had a theory that a motherless child was dangerous to love.

"He lost his mother at birth," Nora had said knowingly of Daniel.

I pointed out that I had lost mine too.

"Ah, but you had me," she purred.

I didn't point out that Daniel had his two beloved aunts, spinsters only too happy to smother him throughout his childhood and youth.

I often wondered if Nora thought Daniel and I were not good for one another.

I never understood why Ernest and Nora kept Helen a secret from me. I understood why Daniel did. Did my grandparents think I'd be hurt? I'd get jealous and create mischief? No one could do devilment with Daniel's decisions. He would see through any game I might play. He knew me, saw through me. It wouldn't work. I simply wouldn't waste my time. They'd presumably been huddled at Erehwemos for months, planning Daniel and Helen's wedding. Ernest even gave Helen away. I was informed by a late invitation, one that I considered half-hearted for Nora knew I'd be away, as I'd planned a trip to the Bahamas with friends that summer. But I'm sure that's not why Ernest and Nora had chosen that date — their friendship with Daniel and Helen had its own momentum.

I met Helen at our birthday party. I was twenty-one and Ernest was seventy-five. Jacob put on a large dinner party with fifty friends at the mountain home of a friend. It was really a sort of watershed. It was the end of my minority, the end of my university days. I'd got a mere lower second, which didn't compare well to Ernest's Oxford first, nor did it compare well to Daniel's first. But Jacob — dear, generous, crazy, often absent Jacob — was the first to comfort me, saying he too only received a lower second. He was at the party, nursing a recent romantic wound with gin and tonics, still alone in the sense he hadn't yet made up his mind to bring someone else home to meet us. But we knew he had his courtships. There were the nights he didn't come home. There were the usual rumours. I wasn't bothered as long as he didn't present the girlfriends to me. As long as they were "out there" they were just part of his myth and couldn't affect my life, disrupt my relationship with my father.

Ernest was shaky and resigned that evening. I didn't take the time to figure out why. I was too busy swishing around my party in my light, foggy moss-green gown, the prettiest I ever remember wearing, with its empire waist and low neckline, and its yards of floating floor-length material. It was raining when I arrived with Blanca, a long trailing shawl draped around my shoulders, but I had carried an umbrella and was covered. I had dyed a pair of satin shoes to match my dress, which caused Nora to raise her eyebrows as she thought it very middle-class to wear matching shoes! She believed in black, white, or beige shoes, only solid colours. I wasn't concerned with her politics of clothing; my only worry was that I didn't want the shoes to get wet, or my hair. I had piled on a heavy hairpiece of upswept curls that crowned my ensemble. Our hostess welcomed me with open arms: "My dear, you look like Madame Manet."

"No, more like Renoir's *Woman with a Parasol in a Garden*," said Nora.

Jacob said to forget the parasol. He thought my long neck set off by my upsweep was very Modigliani.

"A regal Modigliani in moss green." He held my hand to twirl me, except my heel caught on the trailing shawl and I nearly tripped.

I relished the moment. It was in the middle of all this wonderful attention that Daniel walked in with the magnificent figure of Helen.

Helen was nearly as tall as Daniel and statuesque. She had long blond hair that did not detract from her watchful yet open, intelligent face. She was as white as ivory, yet her features were not typically Caucasian. She had sad eyes, a blunt nose, and a patient mouth that was slightly uneven when she smiled — in fact something in her expression reflected conflicting thoughts: her eyes, though questioning, were somehow frozen in patient forgiveness — but her smile lent her face a grace I would subsequently reach for.

"Helen. You are the final arbiter," announced Nora, impersonating Mrs. Ramsey, a routine she trotted out occasionally. "Lethe with her umbrella. Does she look like a strolling Madame Manet, Manet's *Woman with Umbrella*, Renoir's *Woman with a Parasol in a Garden*, or a Modigliani?"

Helen, an art teacher, looked at me with an uneven frown of concentration which reflected a care and attentiveness I would come to know as essential to her personality. She wrinkled her nose, cocked her head sideways, her long hair falling down over one shoulder as she studied me with the dispassion of a visitor in a gallery.

"A Georges Seurat, I think. *A Sunday Afternoon on the Island of La Grande Jatte.*"

That shut us all up.

Ernest sat through the chattering, looking tired and frail. He listened patiently, amused but detached. He watched us for the next few hours, pleased that we seemed to get along. At one point he held our hands, Helen and I seated on either side of him, and he was careful to beckon Blanca so she wouldn't feel left out.

I liked Helen from the moment I met her. Daniel couldn't accept that. I suspect he hoped we'd both be jealous. But I felt no envy, perhaps just a wistfulness that she'd enter through the door into the rest of his life and I would not. I had always known I wouldn't survive the glare of his light, the charge to be my best, the unrealistic expectations made by the faith of his writer's imagination, the changes I would have to make to be who he thought I was, the commitments I would have to undertake. I also knew he would never be faithful. That was a given. All this came to me as I watched Helen that evening, not with Daniel, whom she seemed matter-of-fact about, but the way she looked at Ernest with such a tenderness, as she guided me to his side to cut the cake, and shared out slices for the guests. As she clapped encouragingly for Nora the aging woman precariously balancing her gin and tonic as she danced, listing like a slipping shawl across the living-room floor to the music of my Billy Vaughan record.

Daniel watched what he decided was our charade. Blanca wandered over to talk to him, but he just stood in the middle of the room, looking glum and nodding inconsequentially while she chatted, clearly unaware that she did not have his full attention.

It was after the cake when Mr. Cortina, now just a friend, walked in carrying a huge bouquet. I'd never received such a gift. I considered cut flowers an unnecessary human indulgence. When I reached up to embrace him, my head at an odd angle to avoid the blooms, the weight of the hairpiece unnatural on my head, caused a disc in my neck to slip. I was instantly immobilized, my head exploding in pain. Helen rushed to my rescue, firmly setting aside the bewildered former beau.

She guided me to a bedroom as I clutched the side of my neck and unpinned the many bobby pins releasing the hairpiece. Helen found warm rags and cold rags, cooing soothingly. Ernest and Nora had to take me home propped up on my hostess's pillows in the back of their car.

In the days that followed, Helen and I were on the phone constantly.

Helen sewed, Helen drew, Helen designed. Helen was invaluably practical. She offered to make me a swiftly assembled wardrobe for my trip and agreed to my idea that she illustrate my poems with her drawings. We would publish a book together.

At his flat, Daniel watched me come and go, trying on Helen's designs, modelling so that she could shorten a hem or alter a sleeve, the pins in her mouth as she knelt beside me on the floor. She seemed to have moved in with him. I would tell her my loves, my losses, Blanca's news, my heartbreaks, my adventures at the bank or the doctor, my hypochondria, and she'd exclaim, "Oh, Lethe!" and laugh that indulgent deep chuckle she had. She made me feel charming.

Daniel would avert his eyes, pull on his cigarettes, sulk, and finally walk out.

One day Daniel answered the door when I came to collect the last blouse for my trip. An emerald-green I kept for years, even after the flimsy voile had separated into tired gaps, its body pulled away from the thread.

He was alone. He left the door open, left me standing there. He went and fetched my parcel.

"What are you trying to prove, Lethe? Why are you doing this?" His voice was soft, his gaze penetrating.

Doing what? Did he object to his future wife sewing for me?

"Forget this collaboration. Your poems are your poems. They aren't nearly ready yet. They cannot be published."

"I just came for my clothes …"

"Here are the damn clothes." He held on to the package like a hostage. "Listen, whenever you print those poems they are your poems. They are your vision of the world. You can't marry them to someone else's vision, someone else's interpretation of the world — Helen's interpretation of your poems."

I stared at him. He sounded like Ernest. I didn't argue with him. I couldn't. I knew the poems weren't ready, but I also knew the poems would probably never be ready. They would be okay when matched with Helen's drawings.

"You don't need Helen's endorsement."

"But you feel I need yours?" I snapped.

"Why this charade, Lethe?"

"I love Helen."

"You can't love Helen."

"But I do."

She was an English mother, my idea of the mother I never had. My idea of a big sister, or the kind of woman I would have liked Jacob to marry. Maybe she was that for Daniel too. Maybe it was the orphan in him now jealous of the orphan in me. What were we fighting over? Whatever his silly old love was, I knew it was there for me. Helen could never replicate the odd garment that was made up of him and me.

But the fact remained I liked Helen.

I paid a price for that affection. When I left for my holidays, Helen and I wrote back and forth throughout the summer. We exchanged poems and drawings as we planned our book. But not a word from Daniel. Not even after they married and I wrote them both asking for news. It was always Helen who answered.

Before I left for the Bahamas that summer, I went to spend a last night with Blanca at her flat. She helped dye my hair, loaned me some clothes, and cooked me my favourite Czech dumplings. We went to bed giggling about boyfriends. She was dating a short, quite handsome insurance salesman. I was going to Harbour Island to meet a university student whom I fancied.

Blanca had always advised me so wisely, providing an alternate view of a world that was complicated by the weight of social considerations from my family. She cut through my inherited and often confused ideology with dispassionate logic. She made it okay to figure out fashion, worry about skincare, and think about serious things intelligently all at the same time. It was acceptable, all right, okay, to include the trivial and the superficial. Money and creature comforts weren't bad words. Being middle-class was okay.

We decided that night I would move back in with her when I returned. Helen would sew curtains, cushions and bedspreads.

"You've done so much for me," I said.

She shrugged. "You've been a faithful friend too."

I don't like to talk about what happened that night. The truth is I can't bear to think about it. After we went to sleep, a man broke in through the kitchen window and attacked Blanca. Her screams have followed me down the years. She fought him bravely. When I emerged afterwards, when it was safe to do so, she was like a shredded doll, her clothes cut into mangled strips, her pale skin dazzling with lines of fresh red blood that had breached its levee The man fled but Blanca had no way to escape those minutes. As even now I can't.

We had no phone. I drove her to the police station. One officer took forever to excuse himself from his game of dominoes, collect a clipboard, search for and insert a legal pad, address his laughing fellow players with his bonhomie then turn reluctantly to speak to us and ask a few disinterested questions.

"Can you describe the man?"

"It was dark. I couldn't see him. He was clean. He had short hair. He smelled of aftershave. He was thin." Blanca gazed into an empty mid-distance that would become her new field of vision.

"You say clean?" The officer lifted his top lip as he spoke and looked incredulously at Blanca as he paused above his notes. I wondered what confused him. He then went on smirking as he repeated and jotted down each of the desolate memories for which Blanca was now responsible.

I took Blanca home to Nora after a visit to the hospital where they examined her and dressed her wounds. She shivered under a blanket on the small settee, drinking Milo and listening to Nora's gentle advisories. I asked her uselessly a few times if she was okay, knowing she would be brave and say she was. Knowing if it was me I wouldn't be and she would have stayed with me. If she was all right I could leave the next day. She could stay with Nora till she felt better and Nora would take her home and settle her when she was ready. I knew she was far from ready when I caught my flight in the morning.

Eight weeks later — on and off a boat, after many pounds of ganja and the insatiable, exuberant, tireless ordinary sex of the young — I returned home. My world had changed in my absence.

Blanca was gone.

Blanca had left a harmless message on Nora's door to say she'd dropped by one afternoon when Nora was resting. Nora thought nothing of it.

"She'd drop by now and then to have a bite to eat with me," she explained. "She'd had a bad exam result and knew she'd have to repeat the year. I ran up to see her the next day. Her car wasn't there."

Two days later a neighbour called to say Blanca was dead.

Blanca did the job efficiently. As a consummate scientist, she took sufficient sleeping pills before she slit her wrists in the bath and bled to death.

And later Nora heard from Blanca's sister that the insurance salesman had left her after the break-in saying he couldn't deal with it all. All what, she asked? He had shuddered with distaste as though something was sullied.

"*Couldn't deal with it all,*" seethed Nora. "Pathetic! Had I known, I would have wrung his bloody neck."

"He was always a creep," I said. Blanca never had luck with men.

Within twenty-four hours of my return the rest of my world came crashing down. Ernest, who had been failing all summer, had slipped into a coma and waited long enough for his last hair-brushing from me. Minutes later, he died.

The next time I visited Erehwemos the calabash was still swinging its message.

Nora was staunch and wild-eyed, hanging on for dear life,

consumed alternately by anger and sorrow.

Daniel, fellow traveller to Erehwemos, had pulled up anchor. He'd gone without a word to me. What few possessions he'd had he gave to Nora and Henny, taking with him only his special books and Ernest's interviews and partial manuscript, as though shoring up the old man against total oblivion.

He'd left with his new wife for her native England.

Helen had left the mock-up of my manuscript — my poems opposite her drawings — each page dividing the text from the drawing with a sheet of ghostly tracing paper. For me, her drawings provided a welcome distraction from my poems. As if all that was left of an era was the diligent, patient, line-perfect spirit of Helen forgiving my sloppy literary attempts.

Bereft of mentor and editor, I printed the damn book anyway.

Now here we were, as though the decades had washed us up on an indifferent shore, and even the books we planned so seriously to write had lost their significance and been replaced. I had stolen Daniel's theme, his hero and even his use of prose, while he had turned his awe, his fascination and fastidious mind to a sailor from a long-gone age.

Daniel didn't say much. He sat, looking at Othello who, with Aesop gone, had wandered all the way along the cliff to where we sat, keeping a kind of vigil, walking out to the edge of the promontory to peruse the horizon like a worried parent at curfew. I kept reassuring him "Aesop will soon be back," which he simply ignored coming from me. He didn't settle down till he heard the *zzzhhhuuuurrr* of the ferry's engine. And then he pretended to be unconcerned when Aesop disembarked and climbed the stairs. His was a practised indifference to Aesop's homecoming.

"I still can't think about it. She had tidied the house and arranged her belongings into piles each tagged with a name, her mother's, her sister's, mine. I got most of her clothes."

"We are dangerous to love," I added.

"No. We're the strong ones. The strong have to do the grieving. You told me that."

Daniel was cleaning his grimy glasses with the hem of his T-shirt. He held them up to the light, considering each lens one at a time.

"Maybe if she'd lived, she'd have married some mean-spirited European and had a miserable life."

"Perhaps. But maybe she wouldn't."

DANIEL ◎

I can't remember the exact date of my return to Trinidad to visit my father and the aunts. It was shortly before I got married. I wanted to be there, for I had been deprived of the rich food of Carnival for too long. I had that nagging feeling that if I waited much longer I might not see them again.

Lethe began a restless pattern of travel that persisted. I saw little of her in her final year. She was always flying off with friends — Barbados, Bahamas. She graduated and took a job teaching English at a high school in Kingston, but would take off as soon as the school term ended. She was an "excellent teacher," according to Nora, who saw her granddaughter only in superlatives. She'd got off to a good start as she loved her subject, and though not generally given to patience, she could be patient in the extreme when she wished to explain or persuade. Also an obsessive, especially about order, I knew first-hand she bossed around anyone she could. A classroom would be ideal for her. She was happiest when busy.

Out of touch with her, I was seeing Helen, whom Ernest and Nora had welcomed like family. Lethe had outgrown Mr. Cortina, but I knew she wasn't interested in me as a partner. She had her own car and I believe she was sharing a flat with Blanca. From time to time I'd run into her at Nora's with other versions of Mr. Cortina. She was still my friend in her tense, sometimes sustaining, sometimes draining way, turning to me when hurt or upset — usually with her father or Nora or both — though seldom taking my advice.

My project with Ernest had shifted subtly over time from my helping him to write his memoir to him helping me to write his biography. He thought both ideas self-serving. I had begun to tape my interviews with him. I collected his papers and writings. I began the preliminary research and notes necessary for the book. I never actually had his verbal blessing, but despite his reluctance I forged ahead, believing in the project. We had finally reached a stage where he felt it was inevitable. I think he was hoping it would get written without him. It was an ambitious task for a first book and I was constantly reminded by people with whom I spoke that I wasn't a Jamaican, which personally I didn't think had anything to do with writing a biography about a man whose qualities were human and whose contribution was both regional and universal. I was young and idealistic. He was an interesting Caribbean man and I wanted to tell his story.

Lethe wasn't updated about the progress of the book at that stage, but not because I meant to keep it from her. I seldom saw her and assumed Nora or Ernest would have kept her apprised of all developments. Nor did I tell her about Helen or my intention to marry. Again, it was easier for me if I simply assumed Nora would take care of this matter. I only found out about Blanca years later when I returned to Jamaica. It's impossible to imagine what that experience must have done to Lethe. Her attachment to Blanca was so very strong. It's funny how we cherry-pick the information we share, by deliberately, conveniently, or inadvertently leaving each of us with a different and incomplete picture.

Even Nora's recounting could not have conveyed what horror the break-in must have been for them both. But Lethe has an acute instinct for survival. No heroics, just get through, and, in this case, get out. I have often wondered whether this experience triggered her peripatetic wanderings beyond Jamaica, Lethe a little boat tossing about in a very rough sea, the storms largely, though not always, of her own making.

I'm not sure why Nora and Ernest kept us in the dark about each other. I have to think that keeping their silence reflected a deliberate wish not to upset or unsettle either of us. The fact was, we were apart and we'd have to make our way separately. They'd not make this harder or easier for us.

Nora spoke about Lethe's various trips as if she were a child running away from home. She viewed Lethe's first journey, after the death of her mother, as her middle passage: a dark voyage divorcing her granddaughter from her motherland and mother. I often wondered if Lethe's mother may have committed suicide and that Lethe did not know. The details always seemed murky. Father and fatherland didn't seem to add up in Nora's calculations. Whether she interpreted Lethe's meandering as an instinctive yearning for a past or escape from reality she'd not adapted to, I don't know, it's unclear. Possibly a bit of both? But it became clear to me over the years that Lethe lived in countries I considered the dullest on earth, choosing places she could never love. She always seemed half in the place where she was, and half in the move beyond, home being where she could never quite say.

Now it was Barbados. She was living there the Easter of my return. Easter in Trinidad meant Carnival. I sent her a letter inviting her to *visit me next door, in Trinidad to meet the family*. I didn't hear back, and was surprised when I came in and my gentle aunt Gilda told me that my more verbose aunt, Verity, the letter-writer, telephone-and-doorbell-answerer, had a message for me.

She did indeed. With amused curiosity, she told me that a Lethe Strong had rung from Barbados and left a number. Was she any relation to Ernest Strong in Jamaica? She'd once heard him give a lecture on the radio.

I was surprised that Aunt Verity knew of Ernest Strong. Perhaps imagining my aunts too insular, though I knew Aunt Verrie read the papers and listened to the Rediffusion news. She would hand Aunt Gilly articles she felt worthy of her time, time normally filled with practical things — the sewing, the laundry, the grocery lists, the supervision of the cook and the cleaner, the laundress and the gardener — Gilly nudged while Verrie gave instructions.

With my father asleep in his chair, I took the opportunity to make the forbidden long-distance call to Barbados, promising Verrie I would repay the expense if she would just hide the bill from my father. I was still a child in that house. When I heard her voice so small, so high and light, with what I knew was a jump of pleasure when she heard me, so out-of-breath and needy, it came flooding over me how much and how futilely I still yearned for Lethe. She was planning to come. Just two days. Could I pick her up at the airport?

But darling, come for Carnival.

Never. She was unequivocal. I knew there was no use arguing. We'd been through this over and over. She hated calypso music. As a Trinidadian, calypso was in my blood. In Jamaica traditional calypsos hadn't evolved much since "Matilda" and "Brown Skin Gal." Ska had blown away the cobwebs of mento and calypso for her Jamaican generation.

"Calypso is our Greek chorus!" I'd tell her.

"Ours is Toots and the Maytals!"

I had no answer for that.

She was the only person on earth whom I'd excuse so easily, but strangely I believed her. I could imagine her, in all the bright turmoil of carnival sound and pageantry fading away like a ghost.

Where could she stay? Yes, she would love to stay with us in the guest room. Did I think my aunts would like her? Would my father approve?

My father would be fine, although in truth I wasn't entirely sure. Don't be upset if he doesn't make a fuss, I warned. He is old. He had always been old. He was old from the day my mother died. Still, I promised her my silent father, a complete mystery to me, would love her as I did.

With that she gave me her flight number — there was only one flight a day — and I assured her I'd be there to meet the plane and bring her home.

She called back twice after that. Once she asked what she should bring to wear, would she need a sweater? A sweater, for God's sake! To Trinidad! Bring a bathing suit instead, woman! Would we have to go to parties? Would she need formal wear? She warned me she didn't like going places where she didn't know anyone. I told her I knew that — anonymity seemed to bewilder her — and I would take her only to see a few special people who were anxious to meet her. Then the day before she arrived she called, anxious to know if I would remember to pick her up. What should she bring as a gift? She could be bewilderingly middle-class.

She emerged out of customs, listing slowly across the arrivals hall, her heavy shoulder bag dragging her blouse unattractively sideways above a very tiny skirt. She was breathless with a story about a man in the seat beside her calling the stewardess because he was bothered by her smoke, and her surprise that the immigration officer recognized her surname. As always, she seemed a stranger in the world as she dumped the bag at my feet — a hideous carving of what appeared to be a green parrot sticking out. I gathered her up and hugged her tightly, wanting this nervous woman negotiating a lit cigarette as she embraced me, to be mine to keep. For just two days Lethe was back in my life.

We arrived home in time for tea. She handed the ghastly parrot to the aunts who generously admired it, placing it on the buffet. Auntie Gilly liked to bake. She'd made a jam roll. Lethe fell upon it with enthusiasm I'd never seen from her for any food. She rewarded the astonished Gilly over and over with lavish compliments and tried to tempt me with mouthfuls of cake. I'd never much liked sweets, enjoying more savoury taste. That was significant to Lethe. She had Nora's tendency to find Freudian meaning that became phobia. My indifference to desserts, Nora once told me was the result of being orphaned. She had a friend whose mother, like mine, had died at his birth. His father blamed the unloved child, who did not have a sweet tooth. Nora's interpretation was that the child felt he didn't deserve the sweets. It had touched a nerve for though I never thought my father blamed me for our loss, his distance and silence made him an enigma that any doubt would fill.

Lethe snapped at me, sounding very Nora. "Oh! Stop being a foundling and eat your cake." I watched my aunts' reaction for fear they'd take offense. They'd been minding me for twenty-three years! But Gilly smiled through the compliments on her baking, so different from my disinterest in her greatest talent. And Verrie, who was ambivalent about the rightful place of people or their opinions, beamed at Lethe. Her eyes literally danced with amusement and she gave her tickled, tinkling, genteel laugh.

"Stop being a foundling!" She chirped the phrase with delight, and I knew at that moment, not understanding the mechanics of it, that Lethe had won a friend. Verity led the social agenda in our family, so that was that.

That was a risky thing you said to my aunts, I said to Lethe later.

She asked me why. All aunts like to feed their nieces and nephews sweet things. It's how they navigate the difficult terrain of indirect bloodlines in the geography of love.

She was with us for two days, in and out of the rooms of the home I had grown up in, making comments on things I had taken for granted. The small round marble of my youth, found in the corner of an old sash window in the room that had been my nursery. Her delight at finding the overhead toilet flushed like the end of the world in a giant sneeze that she remembered shaking the timbers of her childhood home. Sitting beside *her* Aunt Gilly on her small neatly made bed, showing the ancient lady who was losing her sight how she could embroider a flower in a neat chain stitch, then demanding the little doily be hers one day. The way she graced *her* Aunt Verrie's desk like a small apostrophe to write them a thank-you letter before she left.

Lethe brought new life to the house. She conquered my aunts, who fell in love with her in minutes.

My father didn't emerge from his room that first afternoon. Aunt Gilly said he wasn't feeling well, though I suspect he was uncomfortable with a stranger in the house. I'd never invited anyone home to stay. Strangely it never occurred to me to give a moment's pause with Lethe's arrival. It just felt right. Clearly in the grand scheme of things we were not meant to share those early years shaping a home or family together. It was also clear that for me Lethe was inevitable, part of some long road that we would travel in parallel, in a direction that might not be nearby but remained spiritually close, searching for the same North Star. She told my aunts she was the sister I never had. In my virile early twenties the thought of this girl I so desired being my sister was the furthest thing from my mind. Perchance this was the only way to follow the map of Lethe's geography of love.

The following morning Lethe emerged from my old bedroom at nine o'clock in a pair of well-slept-in pajamas, the pale material as tousled as her hair and the sleepy frown on her face. My father was sitting in his customary leather chair, his newspapers read and folded beside him. I will always remember Lethe rubbing her eyes as she gave a theatrical yawn when she sighted him like a cat seeing a mouse. There he was. A tired but upright valiant old judge who'd walked the halls of justice where few brown men had trod with authority before. Who, like Ernest Strong, had gone to Oxford and endured the entrenched and very polite racial prejudice of the faculty, his fellow students, and even the staff. He too had survived the great unthinkable war to end all wars, a brown colonial islander in a white man's argument, whose horror only seemed to live nowadays in old men's eyes. And here he was exhausted, sunning himself in a now-independent Trinidad. In that chair was sitting so much history. My lovely Lethe marched over to my father with the stunning confidence of a favoured child displaying her maverick capacity for unexpected love and magic that she managed to pull from the depths of a usually unsentimental heart.

"Uncle Freddie," she said, approaching his chair like an actress on stage, having waited for her cue. Uncle Freddie! No one had ever called the sphinx-like presence of my father Frederick, Fred, much less Freddie. The nerve of this girl! "I knew I'd meet you one day. Daniel's very own Ernest," and there, before my eyes, this stern man, this stillness that counterbalanced my youth, this quietude that caused me to hold my words reluctant inside me, escaped himself. To my complete astonishment they reached out to one another and hugged gently and politely. This was the man who had forced me to steal into the world in silence, on paper; his stern presence made me stop my run at the door. This was the man I only glanced at when he wasn't looking. This was the quiet man whose eyes seemed to peruse a landscape that he alone could see.

"You smell like my Ernest!"

I swear he blushed.

She pulled away, joyous, sitting down on his newspapers set on the small table beside him. The thought of anyone sitting irreverently on his newspapers was unthinkable to me and I watched in awe as in easy intimacy he warmed to her. She tapped her feet and swung her shoulders unrhythmically to the ever-present rippling chimes of the steel pans tuning and phrasing as they warmed up in the distance. He smiled and rubbed his hands as she prattled on about herself, about me, about heaven knew what else, till Gilly offered her breakfast. Lethe requested a boiled egg, but asked if Uncle Freddie had had his? When Gilly said he had, Lethe asked if she could eat on a tray beside him?

I left to do some chores, returning in time for lunch. We sat at the table, my two aunts, my father, Lethe, and I discussing the differences between the islands, Lethe going on forever about her pet peeve, "the now defunct Caribbean federation." She apologized for Jamaica seceding but was unapologetic about her dislike of Carnival — to the delight of my aunts who considered its inevitable advance disruptive to the orderly continuity of national routine that was their scaffolding. They currently feared it as a ganja-smoking wellspring of modern, youthful evil.

The rest of the visit has faded from my memory. I did take Lethe to meet a friend who was working on costumes he'd designed in a large room at the Hilton. She was spellbound by their artistry and could not believe they were made with so much care only to be worn once and then dismantled or thrown away.

"How can an artist create something to be disposable? What about legacy and history?"

"Mek another tomorrow, na?" Philip had laughed irreverently.

I thought about that — was there was some basic national difference in our expectations of the artist or ourselves? An indifference to permanence and thus legacy?

"Man, you Jamaicans take life too seriously. Here today, gone tomorrow. That's life," he said wiping his hands on a rag, attempting to pick off the glue that had dried. "The point is, it happens."

"Remember the dancers …" said Daniel.

His crazy girlfriend Libby arrived gyrating like a flour kneader and landed in my lap. Lethe took it all in good humour.

We ordered hamburgers and beer. She drank the beer, which she swilled about in her mouth with a grimace. I ate both burgers. She was oddly relaxed and seemed to fit right in. Despite her distaste for Carnival, she'd cast her spell on my friends as well as my family, gently harassing the revellers about their calypsos which she claimed Jamaica had outgrown. "Have you heard our festival songs!" she proclaimed, describing her island's progression from early mento music, Pocomania ritual, through ska and rock-steady to the new phenomenon of reggae. She conceded the development of modern dance on both islands whose roots she felt were buried in fragments of African lore and discussed the influence of the dominant ritualistic Roman Catholic Church in Trinidad versus the comparatively austere Protestants in Jamaica, relative to each island's cultural development. She had become less defiant, more charming, as she expressed her habitual opinions. Nora would have been proud of her.

A half-dozen raucous band members arrived, bursting in through the door and chipping around the room, singing and laughing as they "mamaguy-ed," jeering at each costume as they tried to find the one they were assigned. Philip sucked his teeth and teased them back with local jibes of "picong" and "fatigue."

"In Trinidad you have so many ways of putting each other down," she observed.

"It's our blood sport," I explained.

Saying goodbye, I offered to show her Port of Spain, but as we drove through Queen's Park it was clear she had no interest in sightseeing. She was preoccupied with some fierce thoughts of her own. When it started to rain quite unexpectedly — out of a blue sky — she made me stop the car to find her a piece of paper — a napkin from the Hilton — and wrote some hurried notes maybe about our rain that she called "cussid" and too short to be meaningful.

I wanted to take her sailing on my small boat but, when we got to the dock, the water was too rough. Waves rocked the boats. She took one look at the little skiff bobbing and refused to go aboard. But she was happy to sip vodka daiquiris from the club for the rest of the afternoon, her feet dangling off the pier as we talked about Naipaul, whose paper world of Biswas' people seemed to be more real and immediate to her than the Savannah, Queen's Park, the yacht club or even Woodbrook, where I lived.

It's strange, I said, you don't like to swim yet you love the sea.

"I like it from the safety of the shore. I like its unknowability," she said. "You send out questions and only more questions come back."

"But we're Cancerian," He replied, resorting to Nora's horoscope signs.

"Yes, you're the crab who likes to swim while I'm scuttling side-ways across the sand."

We argued about whether the voice of the sea was a language of vowels according to her — guttural, or one of consonants accord-ing to me — not guttural, glugging? I think I won for we settled on sibilants as the sound.

She remained determined not to read *Moby Dick*, explaining that she couldn't get to American literature till she had read all the literature of the Commonwealth. When I asked her to make an exception she said *Moby Dick* was too much water, as bad as *Dr. Zhivago* with too much snow that made her cold. She really could be a philistine.

"You love *Moby Dick* because you're a sailor," she said.

I liked that. I liked how she called me a sailor!

But it's not about water, I tried to explain. The landscape of a book can provide its metaphor. Remember the story: it's the person or the people in it. The landscape, the water, are really just the foreground to distract and absorb the reader. In the background it is the movement, however tangential, of the character — the human heart — that does the real work on the reader.

"*Moby Dick* is your Bible," she replied after a moment, frowning at her now-busy fingers cannibalizing themselves. "It's a boy's book. I don't like adventure stories. I can't stand Rudyard Kipling." She could be so emphatic and infuriating.

I reached out and took her hand to stop her picking. I wouldn't know till much later in life to what extent many aspects of *Moby Dick* reminded me of us in the sense of the hardest and loneliest quest of the true artist, the choice of the most arduous, dangerous voyage, the refusal to accept safe harbour.

"… for refuge's sake forlornly rushing into peril."

She shook her head like a duck drying off. She'd heard enough.

"What are you doing in that bland isle Barbados anyway?"

Instantly I regretted asking, not really wanting to hear about some new boyfriend. I sensed no elation of new love, no residual contentment, no excitement. She seemed bored.

I asked her if this was it.

"If this was what?" she asked, frowning.

Is he the one?

She chastised me for being a romantic. "He's a musician," she told me.

I kept my silence for surely Barbados was the last place in the Caribbean one would expect to find a talented musician, though she would never agree with me. But Trinis are biased. Each island is.

"He always laughs when he comes."

"Comes where?"

She stared at me with teenage exasperation.

"Oh!" I said feeling stupid, and also so sad. What an empty thought.

"It sort of breaks the ice."

"Will you marry him?"

"He's married already."

I cringed, thinking immediately of Ernest. How was she going to create a writer's life? I heard myself sounding like a father.

"You're a writer, Daniel. I just write."

It was true her work then was still adolescent, but she had a natural instinct for metaphor and simile, a radical and exquisitely sensitive imagination. Young though they were, none of her poems felt like exercises or rhetorical gestures, poems written for the sake of writing a poem. She always wrote as she was moved to.

We had recently had a run-in over editing. She had sent me a true poem, embryonic but promising, with near-perfect pitch — an inner voice that gently and sure-footedly carried a sombre theme, the homesick passing of time, but it kept tripping on its undisciplined excess, circling its theme, and resisting the focus to aim for the heart. So I sent it back to her edited with the short note: *The poem you sent is good. Here it is, back to you better.*

This elicited from her an angry letter that also needed judicious pruning: *My poem came back to me anorexic and like a late convert bearing her new guise whether it fitted her or not.* Then she hurled a volley of abuse at me calling me the Great Poo-Bah of Port of Spain, the cultural Caligula, and in a puzzling malapropism said I had exorcised — read *exercised* — her lines as though training mindless gymnasts.

But I have always thought there was something unfinished about her poems. They lacked a father's instinct for shaping the mother-made offspring before sending it out into the world. Was I a chauvinist? Assigning gender roles to writing? Ernest thought they needed more work. I wondered if this didn't reflect Lethe's plight, being an almost-finished creation herself. In the family structure, she appeared to have fallen between the cracks. She had the inspiration and indulgence from Nora and a sterner more detached guidance from Ernest. She lacked discipline and certainty, the confidence that might have grown naturally from her father's attention.

"You don't finish your poems, Lethe," I ventured.

"And you finish yours?"

Yes, I finish mine.

"I must have my grandfather's genes," I said. I saw in his portrait hanging over the dining table a mysterious and irreducible stubbornness. He had a head of stone.

"My first memory of my father is arguing with him adamantly insisting that since big was spelt *b-i-g*, *big*–er could only be spelt *b-i-g-e-r*. He lost his temper terribly, but I never doubted he was wrong and I was right. I was four or five. In the end Aunt Gilly became alarmed and took me inside. I went with her obediently, but remained quite sure I was right and he was wrong."

"Are you saying I'm unfinished? So, who finished you? Gilly and Verrie?"

No. It wasn't my aunts. It was something I demanded for myself. I knew despite what Nora said, our fates had been very different. Did Lethe lack the discipline? Did she expect enough of herself?

She said her feet were cramping. She jumped up frantically stamping them. I pulled over two iron chairs from a nearby table and pulled her close, my arm around her.

"I want you to find peace. Even if it means I have to see you at peace with someone other than me — building a life the way that Ernest and Nora did."

I couldn't imagine her companion-less. Worse still, alone in Barbados, an island toward which I felt a great ambivalence. This tiny country where my mother was born, beaches on which my mother lay in every picture extending into an infinity of wordless silences, a mother's voice I'd never heard.

"I don't want peace!" She blew a spurt of bubbles through the straw into her vodka orange. "Who am I like? Ernest or Nora?"

I told her she was herself, not like anyone else.

I shared a funny anecdote of how Nora had recently claimed to a patio of visitors that Ernest was a terrific lover — everyone was taken aback at one of those odd moments when Nora could be strangely inappropriate.

Lethe pulled sharply away and remained silent.

"What are you thinking?"

"Sex is a tranquilizer," she said sagely. "I mean, if you really think about it, it's so undignified and we take it so seriously when it's all really quite funny."

Was this about the laughing Barbadian?

"In the throes of sex people aren't romantic — they are just escaping the world, escaping the person they are stuck there humping. In each ridiculous pose they are able to imagine things they don't even know are on their minds. It's who we really are but probably don't want to be."

I was completely taken aback.

"I find this philosophy terribly sad."

"Well, isn't that Carnival?" she snapped back. "One roaring orgasm to which you return every year!"

I felt the urge to take a blanket and cover her. She had revealed too much. It felt like she was unaware of being naked.

By then it was late afternoon and a strong breeze was coming in off the sea. She finished a second vodka and walked over to sit on the edge of the dock again. It was wet and she shivered a little, her eyes fixed on a boat returning home. She looked small and vulnerable. I offered her my towel and she bundled up.

I wanted to talk to her about Helen. We planned to marry in the summer and Ernest had agreed to give her away. I should be the first to tell her but now feared hearing something hurtful.

Then here it came. The question.

"Does Helen make you happy?"

"Yes." In truth I didn't deserve her and that was not meant to be self-effacing. Any woman who married me was taking on the aloof and rugged life of a writer. Helen made life easier for me and in practical ways she freed me to write. Together, we would create a home and family, I would eat too well, become middle-aged, somewhat contented and respectable, hopefully not in a dull way. Helen was shrewd and bright, shrewd enough to cope with me and bright enough to interest me. She came from a stable British army background and had imbibed the virtues of discipline and patience. Most of all she had a sense of humour. My decision was made, my course was set. So why did I feel so guilty?

Lethe fixed her face into a well-sculpted expression of approval, looking like Nora as she sat on the dock, contemplating with determined optimism a body of water she would not enter.

When we returned home that evening, the aunts were waiting with supper for Lethe's last meal with us. My father had gone to bed.

"He waited up for you," they told her with meaningful nods. There was new life in the house. Even the curtains blowing in the uncertain weather seemed to reflect a new energy. After supper, Lethe disappeared with the aunts into their rooms. I heard the occasional squeal of delight over a baby photograph of me. Once, she came rushing out to where I sat on the verandah, an old exercise book in hand, the king or queen pictured on its cover, with my essay whose simplicity delighted her. How had she dug up these things? Dug out these feelings from a retired landscape in which these gentle folk endured the changes of time with little but their staunch routine as a bulwark. Here they were laughing with this woman who was a virtual stranger to them, incautiously telling her their secrets and mine, not a word of rebuke about her cigarette smoke in either room nor the way she sat on Gilly's bed, legs crossed, tugging occasionally at the skin on her toes in that awful habit she had when she was reading.

"I pick my toes when I write poems," she explained to Verrie and they surrendered to peals of laughter.

Before we turned in, we watched the evening from the verandah, the night tense with expectation as the busy pan drums peeled out their practice.

Watching her so happily taking over my life, I convinced myself she could not be the woman I worshipped for all time — the love of my heart, the sister to my soul — and visit my country, stay in my home with my doting aunts and father, and not add some extra meaning to my Carnival beyond her petulant pout.

"You know what Carnival is? It's the dance of life, a dance against death. You can't deny its symbolism, no matter how fleeting. It has a tragic joy, since death will nonetheless come, which is why on Ash Wednesday they score the foreheads of the schoolchildren with ash, and the dancers will sense — though they hardly understand — that at the moment of dancing they are immune. But you already understand this. *I never saw a dancer, dancing die.* Who wrote that?"

"I did!" she shouted it out with delight, a schoolchild getting a teacher's question right.

It seemed culturally blasphemous that she could be here, but chose to walk away as they were marking the foreheads of the children, something so profound to take place on a fellow island. But she dismissed my entreaties without a second thought.

As I held her at Piarco the next day, I remember her hair a sea-tide sweeping back and forth across my face as she tugged at my neck and told me over and over she would miss me, late as it was, and then as she left me and retraced her path over the tarmac her image remained, contrary and unpredictable yet sterling, always bright in my mind.

It would be many years later when I saw her again. But that day, as I watched her uncertain steps to the plane, head down, moving numbly like a refugee, her bag stuffed with Gilly's sandwiches and cake over one shoulder, I thought of my father's shining face as she embraced him goodbye, her nose wrinkling as she tried not to cry. She had brought him sunshine. She had listened to his stories and told him her own. She had claimed him as a spiritual brother to Ernest, the details of their actual compatibility temperamentally or of a time frame being a matter of indifference to her. I saw him as I never had before, human and tender, lonely and brave.

As she was leaving she had pressed the folded Hilton napkin into my hand: *He survived that loss — his reckless middle-aged desperate last chance at happiness — because he wouldn't let you both down. He stayed for you. That was all he could do.*

With a few stark words, she'd thrust my father at the void I'd lived with all my life. Now it fills with his shape for me.

We rob happiness when we give it voice. So I like to think, though our paths would separate again at Piarco that morning, we moved into a sacred, shared stillness.

Despite all the steel pans and revellers the next day, as I took to the streets the world she'd left was empty. And it struck me as I chipped along … the ripple of the pans, the sweetly sweaty acrid air, the singing rum, the red eyed trance, the joyous refrain only spoilt by the pickled Dolly ascending a passing float to liberate herself from her golden costume and gyrate with naked abandon falling over the side of the truck after a few yards into a passing band of bemused Roman gladiators. I knew the underlying desolation of this gay abandon. Lethe, who had never seen a Carnival, never succumbed to its throb, never lived its courageous cry above the pathos, had said it all in her poem — "a dancer, dancing never dies." Its poignancy brings tears. On Ash Wednesday the streets will be littered with broken bottles, a place in the past; the dancers will have moved on. Lethe will be gone. The children will already live in tomorrow's Carnival. They will live with hope. They are not yet used to these deaths.

With Lethe back on that bland island, Barbados, with her soulless lover, the great after-calm came. For a while I held could breathe her in from the memories she left me in this grieving city that had hosted her. Such a hard place to love this sardonic isle, yet she made me love it. Most of all, she gave me my father.

LETHE ☺

I was in Jamaica, at the university hospital twenty years later, lying in pain again. I had returned home to have an operation. My doctor was there, my family was there and they would look after my sons. Though at thirty-six my pattern of exile was long established, I still felt the instinct to come home in times of crisis or trouble.

When Daniel came round the door I didn't feel any great exhilaration of joy. I was too weary. I did have a familiar sense of homecoming, as he leaned over and kissed my forehead. I tried not to bend or twist or laugh, attempting to protect myself from the severed muscles in my stomach.

"I came the minute I heard," Daniel said. Nora had told him. He was living in Jamaica again, up at Erehwemos.

Nora had visited only once. She was struggling with chronic, debilitating asthma. She couldn't handle stress. Jacob was away, busy as always covering some conference down the islands.

"Déjà vu." Daniel smiled gently, seeing me in a hospital bed again.

"But a lot older," I said holding on to his hand as he tried to manipulate himself into a chair by the bed. His hand felt the same, thin-boned and smooth, but he'd put on weight. His face had that becoming of self that the young lack. It had come into its own. Maybe less hopeful, more resigned. His wire glasses made him look more philosophical, less definite.

"Your glasses make you look older."

"But wiser?"

"No. Not wiser," I said. The air required to speak hurt me.

It was hard to think of anything but the pain.

"Your muscles are sore?" he asked.

It was the gas, I explained. Excruciating pain that not even Pethidine helped. Someone had sent me a flask of mint tea and, unbelievably, it was the only thing that worked.

He sat there for the afternoon as I slept and woke. He poured tea from the Thermos and held the cup to my lips. He spoke to me gently. When I rested, he smoked and read a paperback he'd brought along in a battered old satchel.

On one of my wakings, he noticed me fighting sleep to watch him. He squeezed my hand.

"Silence between friends is an acknowledgement of man's need for God."

I frowned. Had he become religious?

He said he'd seen it in a little Yorkshire town. It was engraved on a chapel door.

The sound of the nurse rolling a trolley past the door must have awoken me despite the drugs. He was reading his beloved Nabokov.

"Read to me."

"From the beginning?"

"Wherever you are."

I don't remember which Nabokov. Perhaps it was *Ada, or Ardor*. I drifted between sleep and wakefulness to the sound, rallying and unrelenting, continuous and imperiously fine, of that great master of words whose work charmed even on Daniel's mumbly voice.

"I found my poem," I told him. "The one you dedicated to L.S.

I wrote one for you too." I don't know if he heard me. Maybe I dreamed I told him.

At one stage I woke and became aware that he had slipped the leash of my hand. He was standing at the window smoking a cigarette. He couldn't see our mountains from there, only a concrete building, another wing of the hospital. My view beyond the room was either an inch of sky through that window or, on the other side of my bed, the corridor. But here we were again in the lap of Mona, where our friendship had begun. This time we weren't on the single path of our youth; we were travelling down separate roads. I thought it ironic and sad that my return to Jamaica would be to bury the first fleshy home of my sons.

"Daniel," I called to him softly. I hadn't the strength just then for more.

He turned and frowned through a pull of cigarette as he looked over at me.

"I'm okay."

I don't know why I said it. Never had I felt less okay. Something happens to a woman when she loses her uterus. It's much more profound in the mind than in her stomach. I had lost my ability to create, to make life. That joy, that ebullience is in the body of earth every spring, and in its creatures. Go out and multiply. No matter how the doctors told me that they'd left in my ovaries, I woke on another shore, a dryer landscape that would deprive me of the power of a reckless potential I had not thought about and had simply taken for granted.

He hesitated, about to place the cigarette he held like a drunk between his thumb and forefinger in his mouth again, but instead looked at it and tossed it through the window.

"If suddenly you should call my name …" he recited.

"… even from the shores of sleep," I whispered back.

He smiled. He was pleased I remembered.

Things would be themselves again. Sun would be sun. Rain would be rain.

Daniel had finally left England after what he confessed had been an emotionally gruelling ten years, but how else could he have lived those years, or any years? I knew he blamed both Nora and Jacob for what he saw as his exile. Both our first marriages had ended, him with two daughters, Marion and Zelda, and me with two sons, William and Thomas. We agreed that our spouses had deserved more than we had been able to give, though I hadn't even tried. We both had what Nora would call "strange bonds" with our elder children, a less entangled and more easily joyous weave with the younger ones.

We had kept our friendship through a life of letters, exchanged between England and Barbados.

England is England. The Brits for all their opportunistic global forays remain as much an island people as we are — insular and courteous, private yet neighbourly, but distrustful of a legacy of perplexing cultures they used to rule at arm's length now arriving on their shores. Including me of course.

I have discovered you were my link between the outer man and inner writer. These became one with you. Now there is gulf between the two, a coping husband and father who wears an everyman's mask and does the groceries and mows the lawn, while inside the writer is so graced with curiosity and joy, amazed by every new feeling and attitude here, by its politics and culture, its history, the face of every new flower and the squirrels that bring nuts to bury for the time of famish to come. How different we might be in the eternal summer of home if we had to prepare for a winter! My writing has turned outward in prose to the world beyond me, embracing it with whimsy and the shine of an outsider's insight. Maybe poems are meant for the young. I like the subterranean me beating like a heart beneath my inscrutable surface.

He loved that word, *subterranean.*

What can I say of Barbados? Much the same as what you say of England, for the Barbadians are influenced by the English and at heart remain kindly. I suspect they're more wily and though also disturbed by a new world changing around them, are brilliant at utilizing what it has to offer without actually changing a mote of who they are.

As for the split between my selves, I am the opposite. Outwardly I have become an aging, rather pathetic social butterfly, whilst inwardly I remain neurotic, scared, blaming, nostalgic and lonely for the past. I am like a child who hides, waiting for someone to notice I'm missing!

Answering his letters and waiting for his to arrive in the blue airmail envelope with his familiar, small black type, I managed to fashion myself into a separate person for him. Separate from my everyday life with its squalor and failure, its boring jobs in sales or advertising, its tender sometimes frustratingly devoted timeline of mothering, its yearning for nightclubs and cards and dominoes and friends and acquaintances, its efforts not to see the years eroding the beachhead of my face, its passing fancies and romances, its hurts and disappointments, its cruelties and disloyalties. Trying to remember to forget missing Jacob back home. I shut it all out from Daniel, except my poems and sweet sons.

Communication about Daniel's book on Ernest hadn't gone smoothly with Nora and Jacob. Daniel and Nora fell out over what he could or should not write and they locked horns. This was not an unusual plight for a biographer faced with a subject's widow.

A book is not life, fumed Daniel in a letter to me as I tried to mediate and untangle problem after problem between them. *Life starts, dreams, ends — but a book, albeit a biography, becomes its own immutable entity. It is art and its life is not human. It is created to possess the immortality that could never be Ernest's. And who are any of us to second guess the fierce omnipotence of that art?*

Daniel won most of the points. Because Jacob and I wore Nora down. Only on one occasion did I ask Daniel to meet Nora halfway. It was regarding a letter from a great-aunt expressing worry over Ernest and Nora going into their future with the albatross of a mixed-race marriage around their necks. I didn't think the comment came from bigotry. Rather it was the worry of a concerned family member in an age when cruel social consequences to their union could be expected. How could she know that Ernest and Nora would buck the norm instead, changing and reshaping their own small world in ways that would prove her fears to be unfounded?

Mediating the disagreement long-distance from Barbados, I sent a cable to Jamaica: "Will you trust me and comply. I sympathize. Somewhere." The last word I added on second thought and knew on sending it that it was a cheap shot.

Daniel knew it too. He reluctantly complied on that one count, but then the project ran aground over other issues. I withdrew from the failing negotiations, leaving Jacob to deal with it. I recognized I could no longer help, having depleted Daniel's goodwill. After another misunderstanding, an angry Nora made a melodramatic, stupid remark to someone who repeated it to Daniel: "He's not even a national!" Daniel took my silence and Jacob's reticence as a sign that we had sided with Nora. Somehow he thought he'd be deported. This was a ridiculous thought. Nora didn't have such influence and to think if she did and would use it unjustly was not to know her or Ernest, the subject of the biography.

Daniel gave up the project. I wasn't aware he had. The silence deepened between us. For me it was as though he had died or as if the person I had been in his eyes was no longer. When I could stand it no more, I sent a silly letter accusing him of having forgotten me.

Please don't make these glib accusations, he replied. *In truth memory keeps what it must and sloughs off what is not vital. But in many ways I am in danger of becoming my self-imposed solitude, and I sense you are scared and lonely. Maybe these are the years to which "we" haven't been invited. Bear with us in our lost wondering. But your place in my heart as you well know is quite without question, sacred.*

I was sad he had abandoned Ernest's book. His intuition about me was right. I was without a mate for the first time in my adult life. And I was broke and scared.

After the breakdown of his marriage, and his subsequent peripatetic literary wanderings, Daniel returned to Trinidad to write and teach. He'd been away more than a decade. When I asked him why he left Helen, he told me she had become too successful. And what was wrong with that I asked. It meant he would become rich and spoiled; he would lose the edge he needed to write he explained. When I said that I wouldn't be prepared to make that sacrifice, he replied I already had. I hadn't by choice. He said, yes, I had I just didn't know it and had I read *Moby Dick* yet?

Before Daniel left Helen and England, I was visiting Nora who'd sworn off Erehwemos and was settling into her new life at Jacob's flat in Kingston, when I noticed sitting there on the table where he and Ernest used to work, Daniel's first book — a thin red-and-orange volume, a collection of poems.

"Are you and Daniel talking again?"

"Helen sent it," Nora explained.

For a fleeting moment, my heart skipped, hoping it was the book on Ernest. But no; I realized it was too small. I picked the book up and began searching the table of contents. I found one dedicated to L.S. and as I sped through, reading random lines, I knew it was meant for me. *I cannot trace the map of your sprite/your homeless eyes will search but not for me/you will grow old, but not for me to know.*

I read the book in a single sitting, devouring the poems as though for news of him. Most of the poems I had never seen before. I marvelled as I always had at the sheer might of his voice, its power and artistry, its accuracy, its economy, its unerring truth and fearlessness, its fierce beauty.

"He has really grown into a fine poet," Nora sighed. Was I sensing regret?

He was always a fine poet, I thought.

A few weeks later, more news came from England. His book had won one of England's most prestigious poetry prizes. Although this attracted little fanfare in Jamaica, Nora and her friends were ecstatic. I was jealous and proud.

After the disappointment of my shoddy and indifferently received self-published book, I started sending Daniel poems, inviting his advice and changes.

Listen, he wrote. *When we were young, and despite your fleeting figure on the way to Seacole Hall armed with Blanca at your side, and your disappearance up those dreaded steps, I knew it was our destiny that we'd live together forever, nothing seemed finite so it was easy to pretend I was objective enough to offer criticism. But with you gone these poems you send are all I have now, small spirit parts I cherish just to hold and know, to read between the lines for a sense of your thoughts, for a sense of you. Don't ask me to be your editor now.*

And you, my beloved pretty girl, trapped in your youth both on the Graecian Urn and in my head, how are you?

And you, my forever sweet bird of youth, flown so imaginably far from me! How are you my beloved pretty girl?

I didn't answer, but sent him my second book of poems. Again I'd self-published, this time in Barbados.

In reply, he included a dense review of my book with a letter. The review was a treatise, at twice the length of my collection, too long to ever get published. He had lived with my poetry and thus with me for a month, he wrote, as the rains came *and these days there are fogbanks in the valley*. He apologized that the review's section on love was the weakest, as he wasn't able to overcome an impulse toward privacy, his and mine. He'd felt torn between love and ambition, wanting to embrace these poems as something pure from me and yet wanting to return them to me edited and improved.

That he would analyze my work in such depth was the greatest compliment he could pay me. So I chose instead to think he fell in love with my poems and thus for me the review was more credible than the tender letter.

Daniel eventually returned to Jamaica many years later. As soon as he arrived he hired a car and drove up to Erehwemos to find Nora. She wasn't around, as she had moved to Jacob's flat in Kingston. He looked into Ernest's studio and broke down, weeping, at the sight of the idle, mahogany desk. Ernest was long gone, but his absence hadn't been real until Daniel saw the motionless drawers. He felt a greater sense of loss than he did at the departure of his own father. I suppose he knew Ernest better in the sense of knowing him as an adult. I have come to believe that our dead form a degree of sadness in us that becomes our normal. They are separate when we mourn, separate each in memory, but as they move along behind us in the wake of the past they combine to share a common slipstream, a deepening trough, the weight of nostalgia.

Daniel found Nora at Jacob's. I think no mention was made of Ernest's book or of the disappointments. If Daniel was big enough to visit, Nora was gracious enough to rise to that challenge. She was moved to see him again, expressing regret over Helen. Never having been one for small children, she was quite content to have Daniel to herself and asked only fleetingly about his two daughters.

Daniel's return included someone new. Mary was Daniel's second wife. He had met her in Trinidad, married her there and had brought her to Jamaica. This was soon after their wedding. They were to start a new life. She turned up on Daniel's arm during the next visit to Nora. She was ramrod-straight. Helen, the daughter of an officer, had had perfect posture, but what this Mary had was way beyond perfect posture — it was an inflexibility of spirit made flesh. All this Nora relayed to me, still in Barbados, by telephone.

Daniel hadn't mentioned Mary to me in his letters. I was used to this by now. Nora said they were recently married, and she'd decided to rent Erehwemos to them at a peppercorn rate, which was Nora's elegant expression to say that the house was theirs for nothing.

"It's strange," Nora said to me in a phone call. "Daniel is always drawn west to Jamaica while you like to disappear to the Caribbean of the east."

"And never the twain shall meet," I said casually, but I thought about that. I wasn't sure what it meant.

Once again, whatever "somewhere" meant to Daniel and me, it was devalued by the ease with which he seemed able to share it — this place he knew through me and called so special with some- one other than me. It was special to me, but not because of Daniel. He'd explain that it was the idea that was sacred not the geographical place, but I had come to realize that like my father, Daniel in love could rearrange the landscape to make all the pieces fit.

His letters became noticeably more detached. He had read an interview in a Caribbean magazine in which I had described his poetry as cerebral. Not cerebral! I thought of all his mumbo-jumbo talk of spondees and dactyls, caesuras, iambic pentameters, sonnets

THE BLACK PEACOCK   139

and villanelles whose melodic iterations went straight over my head. He told me it was the opposite but that my answers were just ironic enough, tactful and fluid and not without depth and not without grieving either. He guessed I was growing up okay. I should have thought him patronizing, but instead I dug around to find the magazine so I could see what I said that had impressed him.

It was apparent Nora disliked Daniel's new wife. Mary was a concert pianist and insisted on having a concert grand piano hauled up the mountain, a challenging feat that intrigued the local farmers. The musical strains of what Nora supposed was her straight-backed grim classical music were a far cry from the dull casual throb of reggae from the distant village sound systems, making unfamiliar demands of the valley's echoes each evening. In the mornings Mary would practise her scales. The farmers said her music frightened the birds.

Daniel, enjoying the simple needs and rituals of country life, had bought a cow and taken up milking it early each morning. He called the cow Miss Mansfield. When Nora went up to check on the coffee trees, the farmers were full of stories. They told her Mary was an obeah woman and even the farm animals seemed to agree. Daniel had invited Mary to milk the cow. He sat her on the low milking stool beside the cow and showed her how to take hold of its udders. Her hands must have been cold, because Miss Mansfield lunged forward trying to escape, standing on her hind legs with her front legs pawing blindly in a vain effort to climb the guava tree to which she was tied.

"Cow don't climb tree," all agreed.

I only met Mary once. I was in Jamaica when Daniel had gone to Trinidad to see Aunt Gilly. We missed seeing each other. Mary came in to Kingston to visit Nora. Strangely, I can't remember her speaking. She declined to sit on the small patio where Nora's guests usually sat, opting instead for the old Queen Anne sofa inside. I am quite certain she did not move once while there; she sat as though posing for a portrait.

Nora, who loved piano and played quite well, believed that a rigid spine was merely an affectation unhelpful to music. One has to bend one's shoulder and serve Beethoven, she stated.

We made Mary tea and talked around her silence, which was punctuated by an occasional smile awkwardly altering her face, her eyes blinking sharply like tiny shutters going off in a camera. At one point, I praised Daniel's poems and I swore she glared at me with hatred. Her eyes darkened and her jaw clenched. Nora took no notice.

The day Daniel had come to see me at the hospital, he had left Mary behind. He later explained that she hadn't wanted to come. After seeing me, he drove straight back up the mountains to Erehwemos and found her hysterical. She had read my letters. She'd ripped up his papers, as well as every material she could find and tear to pieces with her pianist's hands.

"The aunts were absolute sticklers for one's privacy and as an only child so was I," he told me. He never forgave Mary for reading my letters. I had a similar sense of sanctity about letters; mine was derived from Nora. She considered privacy a basic tenet of civility and ethics. That was the end of their brief two-year marriage. Daniel left Erehwemos, and none of us ever saw the improbable Mary again.

DANIEL ◎

I know I'm going to die soon. I returned to Peacock Island this last time with the stark news. It was confirmed by specialists in Trinidad. It's this sailor's last trip. I know because they double-checked my prognosis. It won't be long, and it will be quite sudden. The cancer in my lung sits near an artery. Eventually it will burst and, ironically, I will literally drown. Poetic justice?

This is the season. I expect no miracles and I ask for none. My life hasn't been about miracles.

After considerable thought, I have found this thing called death is doable. At least for me. I am not afraid to die. But I am sad to go. I could have loved more, sailed more, written more. But it's not as though I have any huge regrets; not as though I haven't had sufficient time to attempt the many things that interested me. To be fair, it's been enough. To ask more, considering all things, would be greedy. I have that profoundly right feeling that I stuck to my guns, lived on my terms. This is important to me. Having said all that, it's not quite over yet.

I won't leave this bleak island alive, but I must finish my book. It's almost there.

My children will be wounded. They will have to be told. They will hurt and then they will heal and go on with their lives. They are whole and can live without me. I take that as a point of great satisfaction. Despite everything between Helen and me, we managed that job well.

If Lethe knew, she would be filled with dread. She would turn her mind to solutions right away. She would move into her fix-it mode, just as she did for Jacob. Of the two of us, Lethe is to be the survivor. The funny thing is that never at any time did I consider the possibility that I'd go first. I honestly assumed Lethe would die young; there'd be great fanfare, and it would be left to me to eulogize her. This of course is easier for me. Once Lethe has satisfied herself that that's that, so to speak, I know she'll set her mind firmly to what remains of her life beyond. What concerns me is who she will become with the last of her landmarks gone, those who have known the whole of her and loved her despite this knowledge. One's children cannot be one's landmarks. We are theirs. She will have her sons, her grandchildren, and oh how lucky she'll be to have those. I won't know mine. Neither of my daughters have married and I doubt either will have children. They are professional, modern women. Lethe says I am wrong, that I am a pessimist, this is the modern way, they have kids later. She says it's probably the better way to do it. Children later in life. I'm afraid to dream of grandchildren. But Lethe says I must dream for my children.

Lethe lives in Montreal now, another of her hideouts this time neutralized by a foreign language. She hasn't really left Alex. She describes her life as contented. She's becoming the writer she was meant to be. She was thrown off course with Jacob's illness. That was inevitable. But now he's dead and she will miss him. As she will miss me. But she will return to her writing.

But this is the thing. In order to die well, I need Lethe. And not to say goodbye.

Lethe is my muse. I am stuck with less than a hundred pages to go before I can die. I know only she can wring this thing out of me without even knowing that is her purpose for being here. I also know I can't let her know I am dying or she'd start trying to save me, leaving me no room to write. Ironically, Jacob's death is my gift.

I never doubted she would come to me and I had to see her once more. Although in the past I was accustomed to and disappointed by her sudden changes of mind and heart and plans, I knew she would keep this promise. And though I tried to keep to my schedule, I found myself daydreaming about her being with me at last, my fellow writer in my house.

Her sheer energy excites and inspires me, even her grief. She always finds some distraction. This time there is an island of them. And yet in all her sorrow and exhaustion she manages to make Peacock Island hers, seeming to engage her spirit with all her natural curiosity and untameable enthusiasm. Despite herself, she still carries a delight for the world, one that nothing has managed to quell. So it's become my task to circumvent her grief with distractions.

I know I am being selfish, but writing demands we be so. I will try to feed her creativity like a bird bringing straw for her to build a nest. To my amazement her fascination is the peacocks, especially Othello, who dotes on her. And I find it consoling that because of them she hasn't the chance to wake up sad.

I don't know why I told her that tale about the peacocks. Aesop told me — I have no idea if it's a myth or not, but she loves magic.

And here she is at last after a journey of years, come to me in my castle, my windmill with the waiting arms. In her grief, my welcome cannot be unboundedly joyous, yet I feel as I had in my first flat in Jamaica, at my family home in Trinidad, and now here on this normally withdrawn island — with Lethe's arrival everything comes alive with brighter meaning for me, my new ritual breathing to mala beads, even at my end, even in her sorrow.

LETHE ⟲

When Nora died, I felt my heart literally clench and stop. It gave up. Not its beating but its potency, its willing me along. It just hurt and hurt. That is how a heart breaks. I was drenched with inconsolable grief for two years, two years in which the only thing that motivated me almost insanely was trying to keep her memory alive. She was my mother, her loss somewhat different to the loss of Ernest. Ernest's introduced me to grief and gave me a knowledge of sadness I feel to this day. Losing him was like losing my way. With Nora's death, my spirit dissipated into a universe of unchartered loneliness, a motherless place that I'd owned but never known before.

I had remarried. Alex, a Canadian, a journalist and frustrated chef. I had met him in Barbados soon after my operation. We were married two years later. The wedding was held in Jamaica only nine months before Nora's death. I had hardly settled into Alex's Montreal apartment when the call came early one morning.

Nora was dead. I was forty.

Alex is a man who sighs. A quiet, thoughtful man. A reader, a skeptic, a sad man. He never had his own children and accepted my sons slowly and with difficulty, but over time he accommodated us as best he could. He always fed us well. Most of all he valued my mind; he was astonished I could quote from Swinburne. Having a dry, stylistically pristine writing workaday ten-second-clip style, he was secretly working on a cookbook whilst envying my less conventional creativity.

An only child of Russian immigrants, Alex was locked into the doom of his parents' circumstances. I couldn't cheer him and he couldn't cheer me, but when I was lonely in a new city, lost without the English language and having no friends, my elder son in university and my younger in boarding school, both in the Caribbean, he thoughtfully bought me my first computer with modest winnings from a lottery ticket with five of the six numbers.

He urged me to write prose, but I knew I couldn't sustain anything longer than the brief spontaneous creative spurts of my poems.

Alex accompanied me to Nora's funeral. I was sobbing uncontrollably most of the time, feeling my grandmother still there with me in Jacob's house. How could she have left? Who would be there to love me when I made a mess, forgive me when I was less than myself, defend me when I was wrong?

A farmer who tended Erehwemos had seen the Calabash in the house spinning for days before she left. She was now manifest in each mysterious circumstance — a lizard falling or an earthbound black crow that kept walking through a low garden bed of phlox and impatiens and the plumbagos she loved. I don't remember much, but there is one short scene I could never forget.

It was Daniel. Daniel walking in to see me. I don't think he came for the funeral, I think he just happened to be in the island on a visit. I had told Alex about Daniel who sat forever young in a frame on my desk leaning against a small canoe on a beach, describing our relationship as special, Daniel as my literary mentor.

"I thought I was your mentor," he'd said.

Beyond that comment, Alex displayed no jealousy at the time. Holding intelligence and the world of the mind in high esteem, he had always considered the men in my past unworthy of either me or his concern.

On one occasion Daniel had asked me to send him back copies of his letters he'd sent me over the years. He was writing a weekly literary column that was syndicated in the Caribbean and he planned to write a short story using our exchange of letters. A scribbler adrift in Montreal, not even living in my own language, I was flattered to think our correspondence interesting enough to publish anywhere in any form, and the pleasure I expressed could rightly be interpreted as acquiescence; he would have responded with equal generosity of spirit — that's how it was with us, and now it's me quoting him and his letters. I had no photocopier at home so I asked Alex to copy the letters at work. This was a mistake. It started an argument that rages to this day about the sanctity of letters, the ownership of thought. Basically he considered it plagiarism.

"But these are his letters," I insisted.

"But those he has are yours!"

It was stupid. I had a suspicion he was jealous.

But nothing prepared me for Alex's reaction that day. Daniel walked into Jacob's house and we embraced. He was one of the few who'd understood what the loss of Nora meant to me. I don't remember introducing Daniel to Alex, who'd been busy making snacks for well-meaning visitors. I do remember Daniel sitting in an armchair, courteous, trying to be friendly, and Alex, who is normally a calm and rational man who hates scenes or public shows of emotion, taking a seat in Ernest's red leather chair like the head of the household and glaring at Daniel like a man possessed. No matter how Daniel attempted small talk, unnatural for him, or tried to engage Alex in conversation, even gently flattering him by complimenting his salt-fish fritters, he was met with this malevolent stare. I was mesmerized. It actually distracted me until Daniel got up and left.

"What a dreadful little man," Daniel said to me on his way out. I could offer no defence.

After the funeral, Alex left me in Jamaica to dispose of Nora's belongings and to help with the plans for a drama scholarship in her name. I don't remember seeing Daniel again on that trip. I wouldn't see him for many years — but he called a few times. I learned he was living back in Trinidad with a woman who cooked great curries without whom he said he doubted he'd still be alive. I wasn't sure what that meant; his weekly column, syndicated through the Caribbean, was certainly thriving and the picture over his byline showed he had put on weight.

.I had met this woman on another trip to Trinidad I'd rather forget, except for her curries. She was a misery. She kept scowling at me and slapping her sandals sullenly around his small house. I was used to Daniel's women being suspicious of me at first, but this one I could not charm. Daniel said she was just insecure and meant me no harm. I'm sure he was wrong. I ended up at Helen's, who prepared us a splendid brunch, and I couldn't help thinking what a terrible mistake it was that they had parted, and not just because I preferred her eggs to the lady's curry. I met their daughters, Marion and Zelda. Neither looked very much like either parent, but they looked very like each other; wonderful brown mixtures with soft skin and luminous eyes. I discovered Marion is my goddaughter; they'd probably forgotten to tell me because of all the quarrelling at the time over Ernest's book.

Daniel's reasoning for the breakup had been based on his notion of an artist needing to live sparsely. I saw nothing in her house but heart and happiness and Daniel's books and paintings. It was a place where he belonged. Seeing him visit the things and people he had collected over the years made me realize how alike we were: some essential ingredient that was missing made us both scattered, unable to see or trust in personal happiness. The thought made me sad.

"Why did you think success would change her?" I asked, for she was to me the same Helen.

"I didn't. I thought it would change me," he said.

That was Daniel. Things tended to be all or nothing. And only his point of view was the one that mattered.

Alex welcomed me back to Montreal two months later when I arrived with Nora's bequest, four huge diaries she had written for over sixty years. Alex encouraged me to transcribe, and, where necessary, edit her journals. Her entries were sporadic — sometimes going for months without writing — and they were uneven, sometimes only about domestic or personal matters, other times great insight into the politics of Jamaica. They were compelling to read; so like Nora: lyrical, wise, witchy. Many managed to be spontaneous. Yet they were thoughtful, achingly beautiful at times; silly and funny at others, but never petty. Transcribing them took me two years. I learned to be patient, sitting for hours at a time, no more sudden bursts of energy fuelled by emotions triggered by a sad piece of music which had been how I had managed to produce a mere, or occasionally, mildly profound twenty-four lines of poetry. Nora's diaries required the long slog of typing for hours on end to produce a dozen pages. These diaries, whose greatest challenge was deciphering her uniquely curly and enigmatic handwriting, allowed me to trace her extraordinary life, stopping in amazement from time to time on seeing a previously unknown detail of my family history, a story I'd never heard before — or the truth behind a piece of family lore.

Most of all, I was able to retrace our journey together from the day I came to her, soon after my birth. It felt like this was a second chance for me and for her; she was living with me again, here in my house. So many times when questions came to me, I'd flip farther into one of the books and a piece of paper would float down with an answer. Or a family friend would phone to say hello and this would be my opportunity to ask the only person who knew some crucial detail I needed.

It was a mystical time for me, one lived inwardly. I lost my appetite for anything beyond the work that brought me close to Nora's memory. I lost all other interest — I think I lost my husband. He says he lost me. He was there and he helped me with my work, but it was as if I couldn't see him and as if I didn't really care. With time, I had transcribed Nora's journals and the long period of mourning that I needed was complete. Jacob found a publisher from the UK who had worked with Caribbean writers. My long night of weeping gave way to that Biblical joy that cometh in the morning as I learned the arduous process of editing diaries for publication. This was punctuated by the pleasure I found in choosing photographs of family and Nora's early dramatic roles.

I felt a power I had not known before. I learned to be patient and to remain with a project by sitting for fourteen hours a day at a computer. I had learned to read and reread, to shut the world out, to live entirely in my head. I felt like I no longer needed anyone. I might have wanted them, but I was strengthened by my independence.

When we were in London for the launch of the book, Jacob met us there. Alex walked solidly by my side, bemused by the Caribbean party mood but proud of my accomplishment. Before we were to return to Montreal, Jacob invited us up to Oxford where the university was unveiling a portrait of Ernest. It was a formal and moving affair held in Jesus College — one of the old stone halls — with long tables whose age made me think that ancient knights must have feasted there. Walking outside across the sunny quadrangle afterwards, I felt good about Nora's book and Ernest's portrait. As though having lived well, they were now coming into their own in history.

"Lethe, what is a portrait of a black man from Jamaica doing on the walls of Oxford between Queen Elizabeth the First and Lawrence of Arabia?"

Alex's question surprised me.

"But you know!"

"No, I don't really know," he said.

I looked around me. I realized that it was now the late 1980s. None of these students had a clue who Ernest Strong was. Why should they? All they would know of Jamaica was ska, reggae, our cricket team, and the brochure promise of our beaches.

When I got home, Montreal being home now, I began my own book. The one Daniel was not able to write.

"Let me tell you about my grandfather ..."

DANIEL ◎

She has brought her manuscript to Peacock Island. It's odd — I have been reading as though it was a validation of me. As though all the years of love and faith in her were worth it all. As though she was worth it all. How selfish of me. But for me it proves my instincts were correct and that her heart is true. Sometimes I had nothing to go on but that instinct, but like Ernest and Nora I sensed a capacity for depth and strength despite her skittishness, her need to come to terms in life with the concept of the edit. Ernest would be so proud. I felt an urge to wave the manuscript in Henny and Timmy's face: "Now do you believe me?"

Her book isn't a biography, it's her memories. Within its pages stretches the landscape of her mind, one that is capable of empathy and compassion, intelligence and character. It stands as a work on its own merits, even if there had never been the wonder of a man called Ernest. Her writing has the lyrical quality of her poetry and the moments of whimsy and insight I have always known her for. There is a joy in her writing which I'm sure reflects the happiness she felt living with Ernest in those years again.

I try to imagine myself working on my manuscript in that room overlooking the sea, knowing that nearby my other self is working on hers. It's strange, but journeying so long with her words it almost feels like my work too. I feel as though our ships are

running parallel at last next to each other — as though the force
of our engines side by side will create a wake greater than either
of us could achieve far apart.

We have established separate routines, sharing our lives the
way I'd always imagined as two writers we would. Guarding our
private times, our silent coffees on the patio at dawn, watching the
peacocks reconnoitre the place afresh each day. Our rest time after
lunch. Our early bedtimes, as predictable as the elderly. I feel a great
sadness that this serene balance must be so fleeting.

And then sometimes we talk to a point of exhaustion.

Her latest obsession is Ernest's desk that some lover of Jacob
has painted pink. A silly woman trying to express herself as best she
can, hoping to keep up with her Joneses. Its imperfection she said
was proof of the uncorrupted originality of Erehwemos, which
was now compromised and betrayed. Ernest's mind lives on in his
thoughts and pages, in the minds and hearts of those whom like
us he influenced, I told her. His world could not be betrayed by
a pot of paint or a vapid woman. It was more solid than that.
I wasn't even completely sure he wouldn't be capable of romantic
negligence himself. Like his son, he was capable of having a flirtation
with a woman who'd paint a desk pink — although Nora would not
allow such foolishness. Not the painting of his mahogany desk. You
cannot allow this piece of trivia to send you mad, Lethe; now that
would be the ultimate betrayal.

But Lethe would become quite irrational about this, dragging
the argument along as though driving home some twisted chasse.

In conversation, Lethe's veil of grief gets snagged on various
annoyances. She rehashes her memories disconsolately. At times, she
allows me to be there, a quiet paperweight providing an anchor for
her as she frowns, the edge of her thumb in her mouth worrying
at the skin with her teeth.

This grief, sharp in her mind now will eventually settle into her heart's limitless capacity for mourning. This will become her inspiration. And it will be distilled into the crystal prose of her memoir.

"Never lose control," I warn her, reminding her of Shakespeare's Othello. "Don't be consumed by passion."

Lethe is far from healed. I was selfish to believe this time with me would be good for her. I felt that having made all my arrangements she'd be spared all but the job of getting my book to a publisher. I had convinced myself that here — in a place where nothing is expected, nothing prescribed, where nothing is inappropriate — I could provide the certainties she needed. Now it occurs to me that when I'm gone, she will be dealing with another loss, another sorrow made worse by counting this visit as our last goodbye.

So far it's been comfortable the way quite naturally we continue our lifelong conversation. We have spoken about Ernest and Nora, and her memoir. We have discussed areas where she needs to tighten or expand. I've written some notes and advised her that when she has polished and pruned the manuscript some more it will be time to show it to a publisher. I suggested when she finally puts the book to bed, she start the process of applying for fellowships, grants, residencies — a writer's life, lonely, yet with its unique rewards. Bearing in mind she won't have my influence, I'm afraid she'll just fall back into the mindless social life she used to inhabit in Jamaica or Barbados, or worse still, return to the dreaded cold northern world of Alex in Montreal. But I must admit there with him she has been settled enough to allow her the necessary peace of mind to produce that book. How strange. He must be good for her.

The only loss of camaraderie is in our old habit of lighting up cigarettes together. She gave up the habit after her operation. She hadn't felt the urge to smoke with the pain and never returned to it. I don't know why I'm so taken aback. Perhaps as long as Lethe smoked, I felt no need to give up. It wouldn't have been chivalrous to become healthier than her. I am amazed she found the self-control; she's always been so obsessive. My astonishment with her discipline has become linked with my astonishment at the manuscript she is producing. Although I had always thought she had raw talent, I did wonder if she was capable of sustaining the work necessary to create a memoir of this quality. Knowing she'd spent long hours every day, thinking and dreaming and writing and rewriting, for two years until she had that impressive pile of paper sitting up there on the table by my bed amazed me; this woman has grown in ways I hadn't considered or imagined.

Maybe I am jealous she's done all this without me.

And here I am now, dying with my own blasted story I've yet to finish.

Her manuscript is proof that Lethe's emotional solitude reflects the life of a writer and not of a waif. Maybe I can stop worrying over her now. Maybe not. Not the flesh and blood of her that will bury me, but over her soul, battered as it is by the losses of the last years. Unlike me, who has always known fiercely who I am, separate than my family, her sense of dislocation is reinforced with every death. Maybe the boundary between my father and me gave me the safety of an unequivocal distance against which I was able to define myself as separate. Frankly Lethe's decision to commit herself to write a memoir, glorious as this is, may be a relinquishing of her own life in exchange for the past. It worries me how she clings to memory. In her youth she wore a lot of makeup. Now her face is quite bare. At first, it made her appear oddly defenceless. Now I'm not sure. I think it's more an inwardness, possibly a disinterest in the future. Perhaps she no longer needs to wear a mask.

I can hear her at night, prowling quietly across the wooden floor.

I see the flashlight dancing in the gap between my bedroom wall and the ceiling, hear the tap running in the bathroom or the flushing of the toilet. Nights must be difficult for her alone in her room with her sorrow. For me, it is now her room — as with everything else that she's touched in my life.

What she hears at night I don't know. Is it my smoker's cough? I don't think she pays attention to it. But the nights when the cough plagues me I try to be quiet and bury my face in the pillow. It's hard to tell what causes her to get up and walk around; she's been careful not to intrude on any part of my life she considers separate from us.

I console myself that it's inevitable her visit will be intense to a point of imbalance. The truth is that over the years it was ever so. We wouldn't be us if it weren't.

Over the years. What a tiny phrase with such long feet.

There have been stormier visits. Lethe, with her prodigious memory, prefers to forget the second time when she visited me in Trinidad. She had another manuscript; it was her first solo, a collection of poems she wanted to show me. It was just for a weekend. I was living with a woman and Lethe said she didn't feel welcome. There certainly was tension enough to go around. Both women wanted all my attention. Lethe was a wreck. They behaved badly that weekend. One sulked in silence. The other strutted about, throwing tantrums. I never got to look at the manuscript until Lethe was gone!

Funny how the memories return. I remember we went to see Helen, who had brought the children home to Trinidad. She had rented a house not too far from mine. Lethe would meet my daughters and I'd get a break. Helen had made Lethe Marion's godmother. Then a strange thing happened.

After brunch we sat on the verandah, Lethe and I side by side in a hammock. The girls were dressing up and putting on lipstick. Marion was directing a play she'd made up and was seriously and calmly walking her sister through her lines and entrances, when suddenly the hammock broke and Lethe and I went tumbling to the floor.

I mentioned to Lethe the hopeless look on Helen's face when she saw us fall.

"It was such a metaphor," I said.

Metaphor for what?

For us. Falling for each other.

She completely disagreed with my interpretation. If this scene was a metaphor then she thought it described two people who broke the gentle swing of happiness without even trying. Just by virtue of who we were, perhaps Nora's motherless theory, we simply defied any chance at harmony. Maybe that's what Helen saw, Lethe said. Our doom! Or maybe she was distressed that the hammock was broken.

She didn't return with me, remaining at Helen's until her flight the next day.

When we parted, Lethe was convinced we were done. Standing at the airport gate, she suddenly railed at me for inviting her to Trinidad. (She had actually invited herself.) I had deceived her. My thoughtless invitation came with the cost of two lives. It was all a dream, a nightmare. We were over.

"Your heart's an empty house waiting for someone to rent!"

All this was said with her small fists pummelling my chest, as amused airline staff awkwardly pretended not to look.

And yet as she walked away from me, toward the plane, I noticed how much lighter, how less fretful she looked. I realized she'd got it off her chest. Her back was almost straight as she crossed the tarmac, her hair in the wind blowing back from her face. It made we wonder if it truly lightened her burden when she convinced herself I was wrong.

Immediately after she left, I wrote her a letter that I sent to Barbados.

To disrespect my heart, is to disrespect something that you own. It is to disrespect the finest feelings that are vested in you. You have no right to do that to me; you have no right to do that to yourself.

I will always love you. Despite yourself I have found in you the elements of life worth treasuring, the capacity for wonder and worship for this gift we share of the world. I knew that from Mona. In the dark days when you lose your way or when you cannot sustain that wonder, I will keep it safe for you. I will keep you safe from the self that gets tired of being big, tired of the weight of courage; I will keep you safe till you are strong enough to carry the burden of bearing witness again.

I will always be a place of rest when you need one. I am not an orphan. You saw to that. My heart has its people and will never be empty again. Once loved, a heart has its home.

I'm sure she rolled her eyes in some gesture of jaded exasperation when she read my letter, but this was the truth. My truth.

I said that there would come a time when life would stop to pick us up again and she would walk with me, always near, the rest of the way.

She wrote back that she'd hoped she'd crash and had cried all the way back to Barbados. I doubt Lethe cried that hard, for she was very practical in her observances. She tended to feel an emotion and note it, often describing it metaphorically as if it happened to someone else and in terms she thought others would relate to. Whether or not she cried, I knew that the bonds between us were strong. Lethe was Lethe, and I have no doubt from the moment she left, even before she crossed the tarmac, she was planning for whatever lay ahead.

For me, I have known time and time again our story wasn't over. There would always be another chapter in our book.

I wouldn't see Lethe again for many years — Nora's funeral — years during which I wrote my heart out, mostly in my weekly column. We kept in touch, talking of our writing and our children and current politics, neither mentioning intervening relationships with others or indeed our own.

I still ask myself how can there be a great love story without physical intimacy. We've had our tender moments, but we never consummated our love. That archaic phrase is so apt. Doesn't it describe the all-consuming madness of an act so primal, so free from logic, so untainted by the manners and control of centuries of civilization that it needs the fire and form of ritual? And apt in the sense of the ultimate, the purity of its instinct, the surety of itself as to what it is, and what it isn't, its sheer binding undeniability.

I am still aroused seeing Lethe at fifty in her black swimsuit. It was a surprise to see how soft her body has become. Not fat. Just not bony, as she had been at thirty. Her stomach is like a tender whale belly to touch. Her thighs heavier and motherly. Her body now approachable in a way it had not appeared before.

Lethe once said — probably to placate me — that some loves endure and are paradoxically made whole by chastity. I know that I never intended this to be so. I lusted after Lethe from the moment I set my eyes on her. In my imagination I have known her body over and over in every way that it is possible to know a woman. But I do think that if we were to last there was something about our lives, if not in our beings, that demanded a sacrifice of us. Otherwise we would have been too human. It might have dissipated us, made us less than we had to be to sustain each other. Who said the world is too much with us? Too many mundane things, the plumber to call, the nappy to change, jobs lost, the hunger pains of disappointments. And yes, that is a glory for some, but with us there was always this calling of something else so demanding and specific: our writing.

And what we needed to save for one another might have been spoiled by the ripening years of living life together.

Did she sell me this bill of goods? Probably this is how I now console myself.

Several times at night I've gone to check on Lethe and found she needed me. Her bed is just a single, so she follows me back into my room, trailing the soft cotton coverlet she's taken a shine to in a childish manner. In my larger bed, she wraps herself around me with such intensity I've become familiar with her softening thighs and her softened belly. I am a man. I want her. But I know Lethe's grief would make sexual intimacy a blasphemy; in some convoluted way, it would feel like fucking Jacob.

But there's more — some deeper fear that's stopped me. I always wondered if Lethe, who would write the most suggestive letters, who would wrap herself around my body as easily as she did around my heart and yet manage to make it all so tentative, so reversible and withdrawable, if she would finally laugh at me, reject me? Would she evaporate like a spectre, leaving me to discover she'd never been there at all?

I remain tentative, knowing our time together carries the fault line that runs beneath our common ground. In this new incarnation, the shape of the trouble is Mamta. If I knew what it was I feared, whether Lethe could see or not see, hear or not hear what I think I am seeing and hearing, it would solve the mystery. Aesop asks if it's my conscience.

Lethe knows what she knows, but says nothing.

LETHE ◎

I was sitting at Daniel's desk, trying to compose a letter. I'd made the decision to leave. Daniel wouldn't be surprised. "I knew you'd go," he'd say matter-of-factly, as though we'd been fishing and it was time for me to gather up the tackle and go home. I always leave. That's what I do best. We both knew the time had come.

Daniel had gone to Battle Beach — it was a good place to swim — and I had asked to use his typewriter. He thoughtfully left paper and corrector ink out for me. I had recently moved from a Selectric to my first computer. The manual keys now felt so heavy as I pushed down on them in a dead slow hunt-and-peck. Any sentimentality about the old manual typewriter as a time machine faded.

Light filtered in through the brightly coloured stained-glass window, the endless dust and DDT forming constellations in its shafts. But I didn't feel like writing. Distracted, I looked around the room, measuring in my mind how much time it would take to finish dusting the shelves, wishing I'd had time to finish it. Maybe it was a task I shouldn't have taken on, knowing how unfinished unfinished things left me feeling. It was the simple completion of a mindless routine I wished I could take home with me.

I picked up the duster and started along a new shelf filled with bound encyclopedias, brown with gold writing. *Harvard Classics: The*

Five-Foot Shelf of Books. I looked at the shelf. They filled it and used up a quarter of the one underneath. Was it really five feet of pages? As I dusted, I counted them out. Fifty-one books, from number one, Franklyn Woolman Penn, through number twenty-eight, English Essays, on to number forty, Chaucer to Gray, forty-six and forty-seven, Elizabethan Drama. I returned to the start of the lower shelf, dropped the duster, and pulled out forty-two, English Poetry, Tennyson to Whitman. The inside of its front cover was dutifully stamped with *House Library Loyola College, Montreal*. Had Esopus been to my new hometown? Was Loyola missing its precious collection before it became incorporated into Concordia? I looked to see what year it was published and found the name of the publishers: P.F. Collier & Son, New York. The earliest copyright was 1910. I wondered what had ever happened to the Son. Did he echo his father, Mr. P.F. Collier, down the years?

In the corner at the end of the lower shelf I noticed a black peacock feather tucked away. It had to be Othello's. Nora had said that peacock feathers in a house were bad luck. Reaching for it, I discovered its spine stuck between the pages of a thin book, the last on the shelf nearest the window. I pulled out the book with its unusual bookmark. Wallace Stevens, a poet I had never read. The broken spine had caused the pages to splay, opening at the poem marked by the feather.

… I saw how the night came,
Came striding like the colour of the heavy hemlocks
I felt afraid.
And I remembered the cry of the peacocks.

I looked back to the top to see the title. *Black Domination*.
I slipped the long feather back into the page and took the book

with me, deciding to sit in the sun and read Wallace Stevens rather than write or dust.

As I pulled a chair from the patio, I could hear Aesop far away, sweeping the yard. The ever-curious Othello walked over from the side of the windmill to see who was there. Othello really was a busybody. I was getting to know his routine. He liked admiration and company, which he pretended to ignore. I would miss him. I sprawled in the chair with the sun on my face, on my shoulders, on my legs, its reprieve of happiness spreading over me. One forgets one's romance with the sun; it surprises me time after time as if its embrace has no memory. I didn't want to read anymore, didn't want to be bothered as long as the gentle warmth lasted. So I was irritated when Aesop's shadow appeared round the corner.

"Is it okay I borrow a book?" I asked, holding the cover toward Aesop.

He shrugged indifferently.

"I mean, can I take it with me?"

"You going?" He took a seat on his haunches, his broom, a stake placed strategically in front of him. He looked at me with unconcealed curiosity.

"Yes. Time to go," I said.

"Othello will miss you." He nodded at the horizon. Othello was now out of view. "He likes women more than hens." He laughed his *cya-cya* vulgar laugh. Then he looked wistful. "He loved Mamta, too."

"Why do you say 'loved'? Othello knew Mamta? Is she gone? Was she here?"

"Of course. This is her home."

I didn't know what to say. Mamta seemed to hang like a dark shadow over this place — over Daniel, over Aesop. Over Charon? Now it was Othello. Aesop pushed himself up by his broom and swept briefly at the step.

"Is Mamta's mother here?"

"Donna? She could be dead," he said matter-of-factly, brushing a step with his hand then patting it as though they were the thigh of a familiar before taking a seat.

"Donna lost her senses. Voices always chatting in her head. Mamta more like her mother. They close. Charon got peace like me. He have the gift of silence from they both born, she first come struggling and bawling, he just passing through sweet and peaceful, staring out at de world like he belong. How twins could be so opposite?"

"Aesop! They're twins?"

"Yes. Two peas from the same pod." He nodded sadly. "Mamta, she loved books like my father. All these book people — my father, Mamta, Daniel, you. They walk in that old room, they don't see how books gather dust, how they come to mulch, all their secrets leaking into sea air. Who cares? Not a soul remember those books, the people that write them all dead. But they care."

I wasn't sure I wanted to hear more. I had the feeling that knowing more would make me somehow feel responsible. But responsible for what? Yet I felt compelled to listen to Aesop. He was in an unusually talkative mood.

"Was Mamta close to your father?"

"Esopus was a wanderer and a wonderer like Daniel. He gave me nothing but my name. He found my mama here with this land. I must be one of his fables! He take Mama round the world like he borrowed her, never make her his own, and when she die of typhus, he send me back here to the land of my grandmother."

The land of his grandmother; this small island about which he evoked a nationalism as potent as any European or American would.

"Esopus is your father?" I would have never figured that, but it made sense. I was sure Daniel didn't know this, though he had told me about Esopus. He had met him. He lived in his home, read his books the way one dips from a large collection, wishing one could live long enough to read even a fraction of them. Of course, Esopus was father to this taciturn caretaker.

"Ten years ago, Esopus turn up here waiting to die. Like he think my mama's land need him body back."

I sat up and put Wallace Stevens down on the table beside me.

"So Esopus was your father?"

"When I introduced him to Daniel, they greet each other like two gentlemen. I brought them something to drink. Esopus told some story about going to live on the mainland and invited this stranger to come and babysit his books like he own this place. By the time Daniel came back, Esopus long dead and Mamta like she gone mad with grief. She loved Esopus. They give her drugs on the mainland that only send her madder. I went over and fetch her back. Charon try to calm her with love. I give her every tea in this small forest. But sometimes it's like she haunted walking up and down. She never stop talk, not even at night to sleep. I send her over there on Battle Beach to stay in her mother's house with a lady who nurse her mother before she die. Mamta loved water. She lived on the beach as a child. She was like a mermaid. I thought her element would cure her."

I was listening for the unharmonious snorting of the old car, hoping Daniel would return. Aesop was slumped as though he'd given up whatever pretense of anger and exasperation he held toward the world. He was a man, sitting with his grief.

"She was a strong swimmer so I know when the old lady call me and say she disappear and leave her shoes on the beach, she not coming back. But Charon, who never shed a tear for their mother, gone there every day to look for his sister for hours, then for days, then for weeks. Then I see he bury her in his heart for he stop searching the beach, stop staring out at the empty sea. You'd think he found her."

"What does Daniel think has happened to her?"

"I don't know. He goes down to Battle Beach. Sometimes he there for hours, shading his eyes like he expect her to swim up from the horizon. Say he looking for Columbus! How he knows that's the gate she pass through to leave this world I don't know. I never tell him anything and Charon, he never talking. I ask myself what Daniel know. He hiding something about my daughter. Let her haunt him."

Aesop cackled knowledgably. I was doomed to hear the story.

Charon hadn't wanted Daniel to come back but Aesop said he didn't care really as it would save him having to look after the house and Esopus' books. He knew Esopus was on his way out. Esopus he said was a writer too, adding bitterly, "like that make a man a man."

"That's the last home all those little paper philosophers going have right there in the sea spray sticking them millions of pages together. Is so empire fall."

I ignored his bitter remark.

"Aesop, tell me about the peacock in the library window?"

"I don't know," he said and spat at his feet. "It always there." He pulled a weed from beside the step, but shook out the earth and lay it down gently on the patio behind him as though he planned to plant the weed elsewhere.

"After you no tourist. We not no tourist island. Why you want to know?"

I shrugged and was about to defend my interest, but he went on.

Esopus had hired a specialty mason to put in the glass.

"That room became his church and that window his passion. So, like everything in that old man's mind, he find a way to connect the dots. He say his new dream is the perfect bird, a black peacock. He want a new species, like cross-pollen flowers — a jet-black rose — or graft one fruit to another, all mix-up mulattos, Portugee and black like me, now these damn birds. He cross them on the main-land and I bring them over here for him as starlings on the ferry in a fish pot. The peafowls never pretty but Othello was majesty from him small. He know his place in this world.

"But from the time these black birds come is bad luck. You mustn't play round with God's business. That's nature. Esopus never care nuttin' bout God's business. He fly in the Big Man face all him life.

"Esopus call him Othello, but Donna call him Lucifer.

"Othello all show and no action. He never breed the hens, neither the black ones nor the others, so Esopus arrange more males to come but they not pretty like Othello and each one die. Othello curse them. He's a smart bird. He drive them up the top of the Samaans so high they can't sleep. They preparing for flight all night long. They fill with despair and soon they don't eat and they die. Othello don't care. Enough is enough. He hear my wife call him Lucifer. No more devils Donna say and chase him round the yard with the broom. Only time I ever wonder if I hear Charon speak a word. I sure he say bitch, but his mouth don't move.

"Bitch or not, Donna show Othello de bright peacock in the window. She want to make him feel shame, but as he gaze at all the pretty light he crow like he blessed by a rainbow. It was always going to be Othello or Donna. I believe is all this blackness drive my wife mad. Esopus really get him black for true, crossing it with one black bird after the other, goose, eagle, who knows what else! Where some people get all these ideas that you must trouble the nature of things. Caribs and Arawaks long dead. He searching for them like he can't swallow history and done. He don't follow no law of God or nature, he don't marry. So he left with a bastard like me who don't care 'bout him damn books."

Othello had returned during Aesop's monologue. He pecked jerkily at the stony lawn. Aesop gazed at him fondly.

"You were the old man's undoing."

The sun came and went behind the odd cloud and I'd shield my eyes. Aesop looked at me from the stairs without recognition as if I was a member of some anonymous audience behind the stage lights.

"My father loved that bird. The perfect specimen, he says, watching that big brute march past him every day. Charon his grandson only laugh watching them. Othello never care for Esopus. Othello play de hand he dealt. Eat, sleep, wake, and mad the hens. He never sire one of them. He won't be party to Esopus' experiments."

Aesop picked up a few tiny stones and threw them toward the cliff. Othello looked up at the sound of the first as it hit the ground softly, but continued his search for grain.

"They all got a curse. Esopus, Donna, Mamta, Charon. Even Daniel just waiting for Christopher Columbus like he got his soul to give him back, and smoking the damn cigarettes and trying not to cough. And you — you studying ghosts too. Except for Othello!"

I retrieved the book, hoping Aesop would go. The sun was out and I wanted to laze and dream, not be exhausted by his island problems.

"If you boyfriend plan to die when he finish his book, tell him since he says he's a sailor, I hoping he go out to sea and don't leave no mess for me to clean up. It's enough I stuck with more books."

"Hmmm," I said and looked at the bird, hoping he'd rescue me from Aesop's strange hiatus of confession. I imagined a picture of Daniel dead in a canoe, pushed out to sea. Did Wallace Stevens know there are black peacocks? Probably not, I thought. He was probably writing about death. I'd asked Daniel.

Aesop jumped to his feet and threw the broom at the bird. It ran a few feet, squawked, and shook itself to recompose his feathers.

"Othello, you made of sterner stuff. You'll outlast us all."

"Can I keep the book, Aesop?"

"Yep, you can keep the book."

DANIEL ☺

I don't know why, but I'm thinking of Henny this morning. She died many years ago. I suppose we hadn't kept in touch in any significant way, but whenever Timmy and I were in Jamaica at the same time, Henny would have us over.

It was really hard on Henny. Henny was in love with me. I chose not to know that, even though Timmy tried so hard to tell me. I didn't want to have to deal with it. It was ruthless to use Henny's information to track down Lethe. It was cruel to show my feelings, knowing what I knew. But that was okay; untended, her feelings should have just washed away with time. I had no right to let it become anything more.

But I began to despair of my quest; Lethe had stood me up so many times. Henny was always there to pick up the pieces, to tease me, to goad me into seeing the fool I was, to make it all seem ridiculous, to have another drink, to go to the movie with me instead.

And so it happened. I was angry, disappointed, lonely, and Henny became my solace. How many times would I turn to her only to receive a call or a note from Lethe that would be enough to make my heart jump, to make me forget about what could or should be, what was kind or honourable, and I would be off to tilt against another useless windmill.

It is a matter of shame to me that Henny had to visit Lethe. It was the final humiliation. I tried to forget it, but it raises its head every time Lethe brings up the damn snail. Of course it was impaled. Lethe was the thorn on which I impaled my psyche. And Lethe was the thorn in her side, impaling Henny.

Henny thought Lethe was being merely coquettish, a tease, a siren, a femme fatale using her wiles to attract and then repel me. What Henny never knew, for I never admitted it, was that Lethe remained my vanishing fair harbour. Had I empowered Henny with my information as she had so generously shared hers, she would not have walked up to knock on that door. I have decided I will never tell Lethe. I owe that much to Henny's memory.

Lethe has decided to leave. I am not surprised. With her it's purely instinctive. She shrugs her shoulders and sets off down God knows what road. Somehow she knows it's time to go. And it's okay. But how can she know what I haven't told her — I have completed my story. But she knows, even though she doesn't know, she knows. Aesop will send it off to post today. Lethe will get it when she gets back to Montreal and to Alex. That's something else I know and she knows, but she doesn't know she knows yet.

For me, the ending is just right. This visit is a final happiness I will take with me for the time I have left.

Lethe always takes my world and shakes it from its axis, then leaves me longing.

Once, long ago when I was sick, Nora called. She promised she'd drop by to see me. So it was a pleasant surprise when Lethe arrived instead.

"I brought you a pie!" she said, looking pleased with herself.

She offered me the dish and I looked at the pie in awe. Never had I seen Lethe in a kitchen. Never had I seen Lethe cook nor did she seem ever to want to be associated with any form of domesticity.

When she ate she did it with disinterest, preferring to gulp down a quick milkshake or a tepid cup of coffee, imbibing her endless diet of smoke, which she explained was preferable to picking her fingers in public, though she often did both simultaneously.

"Why Lethe, you baked me a pie!"

She smiled.

And though I dislike desserts, I made us coffee and sliced two pieces of the pie that I remember was filled with apples, for I felt amused by the irony of being offered that particular fruit by Lethe — and we sat down together side by side and smoked and ate. I was so happy. I was only twenty-two, but at that moment my life felt complete. There are times when I feel low, and that memory comes back, and it restores a man's courage.

LETHE ⊚

I must have drowsed off to sleep when I became aware of the presence of sound. Not a rustling, more like a precise bristling. A tensing or tightening, as if there were a fire somewhere. Then I heard Othello cry, and I sat up to see him shrieking blindly to the sky, his loudmouth beak opened wide. He lowered his stare to me, a little shy, a little startled, yet very regal, straining to spread his feathers ever stiffer and wider, the light behind them outlining their fine filigree. They formed a perfect fan, the veiny stalks, the staggered black feather-eyes, velvet on silken lace, arranged in a vast bouquet surrounding his body. His scrawny stick legs staggered, adjusting to balance the weight as he cried out for the world to hear him. I am what I am. The peahens sauntered by him, pecking at the earth, not unconcerned, as they paused to turn their necks round to straighten their own feathers, but they never looked straight at Othello, who called out and stiffly continued his show, turning slowly to reveal his shorter back feathers. He completed his three-sixty-degree turn and faced me again, straight on, his feathers almost hissing, his head like a narrow mask, steely and impregnable, locked into the splendour, the euphoria that lasts as long as it lasts.

Slowly his demonstration reversed, a circus dismantling in silence, a closing down of the show.

"Come on, Othello." I called out. "Seriously now, are you flirting with me?"

DANIEL ⊚

My book on Columbus is the last of all my stories. It is my end.

Now I will study only the sea. The seaweed shuffles its truths back and forth, this way and that. Things matter for a little time and then they don't matter.

The sea is my home, the sea is my mother.

The only coast with sand is on the far side of the island, Battle Beach. Its sand is grey. Somehow, this makes the place more real, its texture like disappointment. I go there from time to time, haunted by Mamta. What was her mother's home is up on the cliff at the far end of the beach, where I believe her mother died. Sometimes I think I see Mamta walking down the beach, glamorous and sardonic, the way she was before her mind began to crumble. She tightens her wrap, her head held high, and turns away as she passes me. If only such a vision were real, true. That would be okay. That would be good. That would release me. On other occasions I fear I'll see some piece of garment washed up amongst the seaweed that might be hers. I am haunted by the idea she may have last been here, but Aesop won't tell me anything. If I ask about her, he wanders away, muttering what I'd like to believe was inane nonsense, but what I know is not. The other day it was: "Brown people got this conscience thing. What would only make white people blush, they suffer like a sickness. I hope I don't catch it."

Charon glares at me when he thinks I'm not looking. Whenever I come to Battle Beach he manages to be there. It's as if he's waiting for me. He parks himself at the foot of the steep concrete steps to the empty house as though he is guarding it. He watches me. If I were to be around too long, overstay the non-welcome I've taken advantage of, I'm sure he'd burn down the windmill with me and the books in it. I've often wondered what he thinks about those silent books whose voices must be like a rebuke to him.

Battle Beach was where I promised to take Lethe for a day, but it wasn't meant to be. Every time I suggested the outing, the rain would wash the chance away. It's not that she was disappointed by the missed opportunity. She's lost in her net of grief and doesn't seem to notice.

I have felt Mamta's presence like a ghost. One day I went to try the door of the house, but was stopped short by the sight of three smooth stones laid next to each other on the bottom step. A chill went through me. I turned and went home immediately. I actually felt afraid.

I know Aesop is enjoying watching me be pulled to Battle Beach and his wife's house, only to come away as if repulsed. He says there's a magnet pulling me to that beach. I am certain he believes I did something to unhinge his daughter and now she is trying to unhinge me. Although I used her name to get in through his door, I never told him I had been seeing Mamta, his daughter, my student, at the university.

"Why you so concerned with my daughter?" he asked me one day when we sat in front of his late wife's empty house. "Guilty conscience?"

I didn't answer him.

"Mamta gone long time."

"Gone how?" I asked.

"Nothing can bring her back to you," he'd said with satisfaction.

Lethe leaves tomorrow. I have given Aesop the manuscript to post for her after he drops her to the mainland. I don't want to give it to her now. It will seem so final. It would be a declaration of something I would rather leave unspoken and unacknowledged. In a way, our work has been symbolic of our time together. My time is over now. I know I won't see Lethe again.

This was my frame of mind when I drove down here. Lethe was sitting quietly in the library at my desk. She's probably writing me a letter to say goodbye. We don't do goodbyes well. They are always untidily emotional or awkward. Because our relationship has been complicated — not only by circumstance and time, but also by our failures to act authentically with each other — its beginnings and ends are more like chapters or a series of themes a writer selects to write about. These milestones are not chronological, events by which we mark the progress of our lives, our story. Our goodbyes seem forced when we have to observe them. I expect we are deliberately avoiding each other today. I wouldn't be surprised if she leaves tomorrow, ferried away by Charon without saying goodbye. That's okay. I know that we both hear the peacocks even if from our separate windows, and always she will remember their cries.

That's enough.

LETHE ⦿

The peacocks withdrew to their tree as we'd finished our evening rum and cokes. The patio had been cleared of its usual laundry, and we rose from our customary chairs as though we'd been practising the scene for years and walked down to the edge of the cliff. It was like a dream. We were shrouded in mist that looked like a fairy hammock hanging over a darkness of nothing. I had on a simple shift, which Daniel lifted off over my head, my arms held high like an obliging child. He confidently pulled down my underwear, my flag of surrender. He wore only shorts which he stepped out. He jumped straight over the edge into the unseen water. The splash made it real. By the moon's implacable cataract I could just see the shape of a vague torso beckoning from the water.

I climbed down clutching the old pipe railing, extending my arms — this time toward him — and he took me by the waist and pulled me into the sea. We rocked with the slosh and splash. My breasts between us, softly, loosely up against him, his chest arousing my cold, surprised nipples.

I felt that safety, the indifference of certainty. We had nowhere else to go. No more longing or explaining or excuses. I thought of the twin rocks on either side of the Bog Walk Gorge in Jamaica. They stood separate for all time, Man Rock and Woman Rock, their petrified genitals on either side of the river. I used to wonder if they had once been together and the inexorable drift of geological time had split them apart. Daniel once told me they were moving toward consummation in a continual drift. That was his fairy tale. Blanca would have said he was wrong. These things don't come together, they were once joined and were now forever moving farther and farther apart.

But here we were. The sea dried my skin with its salt, but he still found moisture for his long fingers. As I kissed them, savouring them like new words he was offering me, I recognized the smell he now craved that I had hidden from him for so long. We unleashed the words we'd kept barricaded from each other. They tumbled into the night: ripe, silly words, yesses, over and over, drunken, euphoric sentiments, my haunches held tightly in his hands.

And then it was over.

One less mystery. The earth hadn't moved, as they say. I was reminded of the silliness of how seriously we take these things.

I laughed.

The moon turned milky and softer, more playful, the way she looked when she followed me as the child I was, looking out the window from Ernest's car.

I thought of Blanca, whose death, decades before, continued to lie unspoken between us. It was a death that in many ways I felt we were, by our neglect of her feelings, in some way responsible for.

"Blanca," I thought I said.

One more betrayal. Would she have charmed Daniel if he wasn't waiting for me? Like a dog in the manger I didn't want him, but she couldn't have him. I knew my power. I didn't have to use it. It's how it happened. It's how I let it happen.

"That night …" I started to say and stopped.

That night I woke sensing someone was in the house. There was a moment when I could have shouted out, shouted for help, woken and warned Blanca. I heard the small puzzle of unconnected noises, unaccustomed in the dark, unfinished, inconclusive sounds. Illogical and unrelated. The air shifted uncomfortably with danger.

Mine was the room with its own bathroom, the only door in the house that locked. I slid off the side of the bed in a darkness that was friendly to me. I knew the Braille of that short journey by heart. I slipped into the bathroom, locked the door, and crouched in the shower behind the curtain and waited. The shower had a drop-by-drop slow leak. I waited until her door was pushed open and her ugly destiny walked in with its small, sharp knife. I waited in safety while he raped her secondhand, sticking in the blade, her screams disturbing the air in every corner of our house. I waited while in the confusion of sounds I heard my name shouted time and time again. Did she mean to warn me? Was she trying to wake me? Maybe she wanted to save me.

But I was safe. I was safe all along.

Blanca like Mummy, whoever Mummy was, is gone. I am not. Surviving is its own kind of hell. It doesn't take guts. It just happens. Like being pretty or being smart, it just happens. It just happens if you wait long enough for the screams to stop and you are safe to emerge from the shower.

Maybe we are never happy inside knowing someone's left out in the rain.

❧

I woke up. Perhaps everything had been just a nightmare; we'd all be able to start over at the beginning again.

It was raining outside. I was hungry. I was cold. I hadn't heard Daniel return from the beach. I'd turned in early. I got up and I felt my way through the dark to Daniel's room. It was so quiet. He never snored.

I was shivering.

"What's wrong?" he'd say when I woke him. "You're so cold, my darling. I'll make you scrambled eggs."

But it was Daniel who was cold and still. As dead as Jacob, the wrist mala like a stuttered last prayer hung from the thumb of his half-curled hand.

For some reason I haven't been able to understand, I wasn't totally surprised. There is a silence that one comes to recognize when one is alone and no one else can break it. I think I recognized that silence as I made my way to his door, knew it by the utter darkness as I pushed it open and the air didn't stir with his breath. It's funny how people see peace in the dead. I saw the let go exhaustion of struggle. I stared at him wondering how his voice got away, where it had gone. I wondered vaguely what I should do. I knew he'd gone. He'd written his own ending of our story. I wished I'd left a day earlier.

But you never said goodbye!

Yes, I did.

Last words have their own charged potency. They can do and undo.

He'd left me his dream to colonize my memory.

And there was something else.

Three smooth stones placed next to each other on the sheets at the foot of his bed.

LETHE ☯

Montreal

I don't remember leaving at all. I don't remember the days as being separate from one another. But I remember the endless full moon and the cries of the peacocks as though each morning they were to face extinction. Whoever Mamta was is dead, but I see her as a single incarnation of all women — I have adopted the spectre of that strange figure I now call Mamta Dlo. I picture her along the road, with either a hood or black cotton-candy hair, staring with that blunt, dissatisfied look with which one stares at a mirror and seeing in her what one sees in the mirror — oneself.

Did she walk the busy streets of London? Did she establish herself as a writer in Paris? I left her memory there unresolved.

Only Othello broke my heart. Leaving him there, shuffling on his barren shore, waiting for Aesop, for Mamta, for me? Was he doomed by Esopus to long for a human destiny?

I went back to Jamaica for a fortnight and decided not to take on the endless task of sorting out the dead. Let the girlfriend do it. I went home instead. Home now was Alex.

I had grown used to seeing Alex at the airport when I arrived. He had become family, not a rock so much as a familiar landmark on my horizon. He moved too quickly toward me this time and the furrow on his brow, the awkwardness of his sympathetic look,

I knew he'd heard Daniel was gone. I was grateful I didn't have to explain.

My detachment was caused by an old grief. I knew well how to handle that. It was a fifth gear for cruising down the highway. I'd settle back, prepare myself for another long drive alone. "Death's as easy as the turn of a wrist," Daniel said as we talked of Jacob's suicide. Had Daniel done the same thing?

When I checked the mail, I saw the large envelope from Daniel dated a fortnight before, waiting for me.

It was very heavy. It was his manuscript. He'd done it! I felt both excited and afraid to open the package.

I pulled out the white pages bearing the familiar black type, proof of the words he had spoken.

The title looked so small: *Columbus — The Seeker* by Daniel Smith.

Hi again,

When you receive this manuscript you will be back in Montreal and I will be gone. I knew only you could pull the rest of my story out from me, a story that had got stuck in my throat like a seed. You are my muse, Lethe. You always were. And as my muse you have always done right by me. I send you this manuscript. You will know what to do with it. Any proceeds I know you will see that my daughters receive.

"One afternoon when he was very old, while he was sitting dreaming in the whispering shade of the great Samaans waiting for his death, he thought he heard a voice say, Can you see the peacock? — and, lifting his head, he became aware of the sound of wings. A large black bird flew overhead, its shadow fleeing across his house and lawn, across the chair where he sat like a benediction. The bird landed deftly on a high limb of the Samaans its long tail settling to trail horizontally down the trunk till, in the shadows,

*without movement, it became invisible. He wondered if he'd
dreamed it. It then occurred to him that it was she who had flickered
across his face, returning home from the funeral of her father."*

    *It is certain we'll not see each other again, but we have grown
used to being more apart than together. Our conversation doesn't
need to end because by now we can finish each other's sentences,
answer each other's questions before they're asked, maybe even
dream each other's dreams!*

    Somewhere is everywhere in the world I was loved by you.

Daniel

Over the years I have often thought about this magical time that seems almost not to have happened. But just for that moment there was an "us."

We are flawed and unclean as we stand in the rain. We love. Gently or terribly, but we love. That's what remains.

"Do you know the sound you hear in the shell is really the sound of blood circulating in your own ear?"

Shut up and sleep, Alex.

But I couldn't sleep. I was thinking about Edgar, changing my mind again and again. Should I let him go as Alex suggested? Just another ghost? Or should I call him. Daniel's damn echoes.

I wondered how Daniel had closed off his book. I crept downstairs to the study where the stack of obedient pages firmly embossed with each punch of Daniel's familiar black print, had taken up residence on my desk.

I had the whole night. I might as well settle down here and start reading.

I cheated and turned to the very last page. And there it was:

EREWHEMOS

Unpacking to resettle into my old life again, I retrieved the Wallace Stevens book to place on my shelf. I stared at the feather extending from its pages. And there, bright as a turquoise sea with its navy-blue eye was the peacock's feather which, when packed, had been as black as Othello.

Sometimes, insulated by this city, I still hear the sea as it bore witness for me. All islands are made of rock. See how they wear down so slowly over millennia. So has all the water of the world given and taken its meanings. Isn't that the truth of eternity? A thing that simply is. And is and is and is.

ACKNOWLEDGEMENTS

Wholehearted thanks to the Toronto Arts Council and the Ontario Arts Council for grants that made the writing of this book possible; Velvet Haney; Bonnie Munday, Jane Brox, Jodi Doff, Rosalie Day, Christina Shea, Martin Mordecai; my beloved book club; Trevor Chin Fook; my agent, Morty Mint; my editor and publisher, Marc Côté; and Iz Cinman, as always.